# URBAN MYSTIC ACADEMY: FIRST PROJECT

### JENNIFER ROSE MCMAHON

Copyright © 2019 by Jennifer Rose McMahon

All rights reserved.

This book is a work of fiction. All characters, places, and incidents described in this publication are used fictitiously or are entirely fictional.

No part of this book may be reproduced in any form or by any electronic or mechanical means, including information storage and retrieval systems, without written permission from the author, except for the use of brief quotations in a book review.

Cover design by Rebecca Frank of Bewitchingbookcovers.com

Dubhdara Publishing

www.jenniferrosemcmahon.com

## PRAISE FOR JENNIFER ROSE MCMAHON

"McMahon's excellent paranormal mystery. Teen and adult readers alike will be clamoring for the sequel."

— PUBLISHERS WEEKLY STARRED REVIEW

"Engaging, beautifully written scenes, and idyllic descriptions keep the tale moving at a quick pace. The characters are engaging and they draw a person in to this tale of adventure and intrigue. Adrenaline-fueled action and enough twists and turns to keep even the most astute readers on their toes, this is a captivating story with a heroine who is forcefully engaging."

— IND'TALE MAGAZINE

"As Chieftain of The O'Malley Clan I am always interested in anything to do with Granuaile, our very famous Pirate Queen ancestor. Jennifer's novel captures the connection with the past which we treasure in Ireland. The Irish landscape, contemporary social life, the Irish language, and romance are woven into this fantasy story about Maeve Grace O'Malley and her quest to solve her 'Awake Dreams'. I am certainly looking forward to the sequel. More BOHERMORE please!"

— SARAH KELLY, O'MALLEY CLAN CHIEFTAIN 2017

**URBAN MYSTIC ACADEMY: FIRST PROJECT**

by Jennifer Rose McMahon

# CHAPTER 1

Purple dye dripped off the ends of my hair, creating bold splatter patterns across the porcelain sink. I pulled my fingers through the full length to be sure color coated every strand. Staring into my unimpressed eyes, I told the mirror, "You can do this. Again."

Moving to another school should have felt natural at this point. I'd done it enough times—once a year, practically. Mom always decided to move during the summer months to make the transitions smoother. I was supposed to believe that was thoughtful of her. But the truth was, it felt more like we were running from something at every turn. Our landlords were always ready to call the sheriff, in hopes of getting some rent for a change. Mom wasn't the best at keeping up with such trivial matters.

So, here we were again. A new town. Another chance for a new identity. A fresh start.

No thanks.

That might have sounded good freshman year, but I was a senior now. I didn't need any more fresh starts. I was ready to get on with my life and leave all this crap and uncertainty behind me. I'd figure out what to do on my own, once I had my diploma.

Fortunately, I understood that my education was my power. Without it, I'd remain trapped in this cycle of dysfunction forever, and there was no way I'd settle for that. I even had a twisted pipe dream of attending college... somehow.

But for now, I decided I would stick with my usual plan for my new school. I'd keep my head down, ignore everyone, and just get through the next one hundred and eighty school days to my freedom.

Blinking into the mirror, I noticed that the purple dye made my hair look black, and a twinge of panic ran through me. I just wanted a subtle violet hue over my dirty blonde hair—something to say, "Leave me alone. I have a lot on my mind,"—not a full-on goth-look. With a shrug of my shoulders, I realized either would be fine. It didn't matter.

But then, it was the strange look in my eyes, more than my odd hair, that caught my attention.

I held a lost gaze. The deep blue of my irises was like the abyss of the ocean depths. The color whirled like a downward vortex, making me dizzy, and I shook my head to steady it. I stared into the mirror again and gasped as a stranger stared back at me, searching like they were struggling to find a way out.

I squeezed my eyes shut. The reflection had been my own, but somehow I didn't know her.

A strange feeling brewed in my gut, as memories of a place I'd never been flashed through my mind—an unusual metal gate, deep woods, glowing purple flames.

My stomach tightened, sending nervous energy through me, clenching my teeth.

Then the image of a star surrounded by intricate symbols flashed in my mind. The vision caused me to stand up tall as it struck me deep in my core.

*Here it comes again—my evil anxiety.*

Sweat broke out on my forearms—the constant physical indicator of my inner stress.

I lifted one hand to rub my arm and then stopped short at the sight of purple dye all over my hands.

Shit! I'd forgotten to use the gloves in the kit.

My heart rate jumped ten levels as I cranked the faucet on. Hot water rushed out of the tap, scorching the skin off my hands as I fumbled to get the temperature right. Wet, plum-colored dye flew everywhere, splashing onto the white tiles behind the sink and on the floor. In the back of my mind, I knew the mess would be hell to clean up, but my panic drove me forward, scrubbing furiously.

Adding soap to a full lather, I rinsed my hands only to reveal a blotchy tie-dye effect all over my skin. My fingernails were the worst with black stains under the nails and dark purple lines at the cuticles. Frantically, I ripped open the alcohol wipe included in the coloring box for 'touch-up' and wiped it all over my hands, digging it under my nails.

It helped a little.

But the damage was done.

*Great.*

First day of school tomorrow, and I looked like the walking dead.

At least my hair turned out well.

Once it dried, the shade of purple glowed like lavender. It was perfect.

My hands, however... not so much.

And the state of the bathroom after my Armageddon... a disaster. Once my mother woke from her Svedka-coma, she'd be sure to deliver some sound verbal lashings and hours of scrubbing. My welcomed escape for the moment was school.

Shame-of-the-day number one: purple zombie hands.

Shame number two: no car.

Finding a part-time job was a must, but for now, I had to survive on my measly savings from DQ. It was enough to keep my wardrobe decent and my cell phone activated but far from paying for driver's ed or a vehicle of *any* form.

The school was within walking distance though, ten minutes max, so that was a plus.

I hoisted my light pack over my shoulder and stepped out into the all-too-early morning. Commuter traffic hadn't even started up yet, and here I was heading off for the day. It was pure torture. My bed always beckoned me back at this point, but I fought the familiar urge to return to it, and powered on.

Moving past the lake by my house, I noticed how pretty it was for the first time. I glanced around the neighborhood, seeing mature maples, flags hanging from telephone poles, and a free-library box on the corner, full of books for the taking. It was actually a charming town.

I shot my eyes forward again, refusing to allow myself to like it here.

It was too nice for us.

It wouldn't last.

It never did.

Following the GPS on my phone, I had three minutes until arriving at the school. I slowed my pace to avoid the inevitable, but it was too late. Busses passed me, and a few more walkers filled the sidewalk, proving I was almost there.

My anxiety tweaked at me, and I swallowed hard to keep it down. Everyone would know I was the new girl, and I prepared myself for the unrelenting stares.

It wasn't my ripped jeans and leather jacket that would stand out most, though. It was my hair. Okay, and now my hands, too.

Why did I always do this to myself? It was like I couldn't help it. Different school, different hair color. Maybe it was subconscious since my mother hated it so much. I wasn't sure. All I knew was that I was compelled to do it.

Every time.

And now, once again, it was clear that my look didn't fit in. That was obvious from all the khaki, fresh white Vans, and perfectly-trimmed, straightened hair, everywhere.

But it didn't bother me. It was exactly what I'd been aiming for. As always.

If I didn't fit in, then no one would pay attention to me. I'd be left alone to get through my sentence and be done with it.

So I'd thought.

# CHAPTER 2

Lifting my eyes as I approached the front of the school, I was shocked at first by its gothic architecture. The building looked more like a regal, ivy-covered college than a public high school. I was used to poured-concrete structures built in the seventies, with dirty buckets in the halls collecting drips from the ceilings.

This place was better. Way better.

My mood lightened slightly as I moved up the granite steps at the front entrance. Two sets of stately double doors waited at the top with the words 'Lakefield High School' scrolled above them. My primary focus was on finding the main office and meeting with my guidance counselor for the typical 'new student' run-through.

As I reached the top of the stairs, I glanced toward a student leaning against the railing. His eyes met mine, and he watched me as I pulled on the door nearest my reach. I fumbled for a moment, distracted by his piercing gaze. His stare unnerved me like he knew me or was sizing me up.

I ground my teeth in annoyance. I'd already broken my cardinal rule of keeping my head down and avoiding eye contact at all cost.

The bang of the door behind me echoed into the long corridor, emphasizing the fact that the hallway was empty. Clearly, the students avoided entering the confines of the school until the very last minute. That was fine with me. I'd rather remain unseen in my lost wanderings while searching for the elusive office.

A white sign stuck out from the wall ahead of me letting me know exactly where to go, and I moved with purpose toward the office. Maybe there was a chance my meeting would be quick, and I'd get to class before the first bell. I hated walking in late. There was nothing worse than all eyes staring as the new kid searched for an empty seat.

Standing at the door, I took a deep breath and reached for the handle. As I pushed it in, I lost my balance as the door pulled open from within. Weightless, I stumbled forward and shuffled to avoid hitting the student who had just flung the door open, exiting at the exact same time.

He chuckled, holding the door steady to help me regain my balance. I swore under my breath and glanced up at him. There was no doubt he was a football player, judging by the way his broad shoulders filled the doorframe. His friendly eyes held mine, and I paused for a second staring at him, waiting for him to say something. My awkward hesitation threw me off, and I fumbled with my bag. It wasn't that he was beyond attractive and beautiful and handsome, but it was the fact that I'd looked at him at all.

What was the matter with me? I was breaking my first steadfast rule left and right. Keep head down, ignore everyone—was it really that hard?

It was weird, though, none of the other students drew my attention, but with those two guys, I couldn't help myself. It was like we already knew each other. It was the first time I ever felt anything like that before when entering a new school.

I pulled my gaze away, frustrated by my error, and focused on the desk ahead of me. The secretary watched with an annoying smirk like she'd caught me blushing or something. She dragged her pencil through her short, spiky hair, waiting for me to pull myself together.

*Damn it.*

I had to stop having eye contact with the students here. I was usually a master at avoidance, but clearly, something about Lakefield was making me crazy, throwing me off my game.

I'd have to try harder if I was planning on surviving my final year. Making connections of any form was not a part of my master plan.

"Can I help you?" the secretary probed. Her blank stare and monotone proved how much she loved her job. I half-expected her to snap on gum.

"I'm new here," I replied. "Brynn Douglas."

"Do you have an appointment?" she murmured.

"Umm, no. I didn't realize I needed one." I struggled to keep my tone civil. Her attitude was already grating on me. "I think my records were sent over."

She rolled her eyes.

"Have a seat." She let out a deep sigh as she pushed herself up from her chair. "I'll see who your counselor is."

She shuffled along a row of office doors and stopped outside the one at the end. After a few words, she headed back, taking her time for fear I might actually think she cared about me.

"Ms. Kelly can see you," she said, motioning her head in the direction of the office.

*Obviously.*

It's not like they'd leave a new student just hanging around. Didn't this woman know the drill?

But instead, I swallowed my cynicism and remained calm.

"Thanks," I forced the word and walked down the narrow hallway to Ms. Kelly's office.

I had no idea what to expect. I'd had so many different teachers and counselors throughout high school. Sadly, I expected the worst.

My last guidance counselor was an old dude. A hippy. He was nice enough but never stayed focused on what I needed. He was too busy talking about himself with a load of 'back-in-my-day' crap. I never went to him for anything after our first meeting, no matter how much I needed help.

"Hi. You must be Brynn," Ms. Kelly's friendly voice invited me in.

My eyes widened at the sight of her. She wasn't too young, but young enough that she was still vibrant and full of positive energy. I was a little surprised at how cool she seemed.

"Um, yeah."

"Come on in. I've been looking forward to meeting you," she said.

"Really?" I mumbled under my breath.

"Yes. Have a seat." She gestured to several options.

There was a chair right in front of her desk, one off to the side by the fidget toys, and another against the wall by the colorful pictures of former students, intriguing field trips, and amateur artwork. I sat in the chair directly in front of her without hesitation.

She smiled and continued. "Your transcript kept me busy," she teased. "It's choppy, with different variations depending on each school you've attended." She scanned the multiple pages.

My heart rate accelerated. This was the part where the counselor always challenged my credits or tried to put me in the grade below me. I mean, I was eighteen. Could it be more obvious that I was a senior? Either way, this moment was never smooth, and I prepared myself for the fight.

"It's clear to me, though," she added, "you're an exceptional student."

The breath I'd been holding since entering her office released from me in a long whoosh.

"Um, thank you," I whispered, still waiting for the other shoe to drop.

"At first, I was concerned that you had requested all AP courses, but after reviewing your academic records, I can see why. It appears that learning is one of your strengths." She watched me for a response.

I'd never considered having any strengths before, but somehow, the way she said it made it sound like a compliment. I had no idea how to react to it.

"I guess."

Maybe it was true. I had nothing else to focus on, so it made sense my school work would get my full attention. But the more I thought about it, the more I realized that learning *did* come easy to me. The other students always had questions and struggled on the tests while I sailed through every hoop. It was one small blessing, I supposed.

Ms. Kelly gazed at me like she was trying to figure me out. But it was more than that. She looked into my soul like she could see more of me than I wanted to allow. I pulled my eyes away from her, feeling like it was my only way of hiding my true self. Her examination was unsettling, to say the least.

"Well, typically, I would be hesitant about having a new student take five AP classes, but judging from your perfect scores on last year's exams, I think you've got this." She smiled.

I couldn't believe it. It was the first time a counselor had faith in me. Last year's hippy made me sign over-ride forms and practically swear away my firstborn to take their advanced placement classes. He probably never even took the time to see my exam scores. That was how it always went. I was never around long enough for people to see my academic history at their schools. It was like they always had to take a leap of faith with me, assuming the wayward girl would follow the wrong path.

Ms. Kelly was different, though. She was more chill like she believed in me. Her loose sweater hung comfortably from her shoulders and her surfer-girl hair looked like she'd only just run her fingers through it this morning. I'd swear she probably had yoga pants on, but I couldn't see for sure. Her pretty face was non-judgmental, and I felt comfortable in her presence, even with her uncanny ability to stare straight into my naked soul. It was clear, I needed more armor.

She studied me with one eye squinted. "You forgot to wear gloves, right?"

I clasped my hands together and hid them between my knees. "Oh, um, yeah. Nerves, I guess."

"There's no way you can walk into class like that," she chuffed.

My face burned as I fought her surprising criticism.

"Here," she said, handing me a pump bottle of organic oil hand-lotion. "This stuff works magic! I use it on my hands all the time, and it's amazing." Her face lit up to the point of no refusal.

I squirted a generous amount of the white lotion onto my palms and rubbed it all over. She handed me a bunch of tissues, and I wiped all the purple-tinted mess off my hands.

"Oh my god. That's so much better," I gasped. "Thank you."

Most of the purple staining had lifted, leaving only a slight hue on my skin. The nails weren't great, but I could live with that. I relaxed ten-fold now, knowing I wouldn't be seen as a freak the moment I walked into class. Well, not a total freak.

I glanced up at her with gratitude splashed across my face. I mean, seriously, she's the first person who ever actually helped me on the first day of school. Like, *actually* helped me.

Then she said, "You're a sensitive person, aren't you?"

I pulled back.

Suddenly I wasn't so comfortable in her presence. She picked up on too much like she could read me.

I wasn't used to people prying into my privacy and asking me if I was an emotionally frail person. That was crossing the line. What the hell? Did I look like I was about to cry or something?

I struggled to find my words, and before I could reply with something that would shut her down and decide I was a write-off, she spoke again.

"Sorry, I didn't mean it like that." She chuckled. "I mean, you *are* a sensitive." She hesitated on her next words, watching me fidget, then smirked. "And judging by the look on your face, you don't even know it."

What the hell was the difference? "You're a sensitive person," or "You *are* a sensitive." What the actual fuck? All I knew was she was getting too personal asking about my emotional stability, because, to be honest, it was dodgy.

I reached for the ends of my hair and twirled them. "Is it the purple? You think I'm unstable because of my hair color?" I glared at her, waiting for the same judgmental treatment I'd received from the secretary.

"No, not at all. Your hair color is amazing." She smiled with a warm glow in her eyes, winning me back almost instantly. "It's just a feeling I get from you like you perceive things differently from others. Like, you're more in tune with the world around you, more aware." She hesitated, studying me again. "Does the make sense at all?"

I stared back at her.

This was not the typical new-student-entry-meeting protocol. Now was the time she should be asking me about a bus pass, homeroom assignment, and giving me a copy of my schedule. But no. Not this time. This time my guidance counselor was asking me about how I perceived the world. She must be tripping.

But as I looked into her honest eyes, I saw more than the typical routine meeting. Her words then took a deeper meaning in my mind as I thought about them.

*Yes.*

Yes, I was more aware of subtle sensations around me. Yes, I could pick up on the deeper meaning of people's words or actions easily. It always scared me actually, because I typically believed everyone had that ability. It made me feel exposed, thinking that people understood me and my thoughts, the way I understood theirs.

Then I nodded with a shrug.

"Maybe," I said.

"Yes." She smiled. "I thought so. It's something I pick up on about people. It helps me to understand you better, which is a good thing, considering I'll be your school counselor for the rest of the year. It's best I know you as well as possible, so I can help you reach your goals."

"Oh." My breath blew out of me. "I get it. Okay." The tension in my shoulders released as I realized she was just trying to get to know me better, so she could be effective in her job. I huffed at myself for thinking she was diving into my mind, trying to pull my soul out through my eyes.

"So, what *are* your goals?" she asked. "What do you want to do when you graduate?"

I shrugged, clearing my mind of my earlier panic from her intrusive questions. "I don't know. I just want to finish high school and get my diploma."

"I see a lot more potential in you," she said.

Oh, here we go. She's getting personal again.

I thought for a minute about her comment and then realized it actually wasn't that bad. It was nice, even.

I remained silent, having no clue how to respond to a potential compliment, knowing that it was more likely she said that to everyone.

She went on. "Have you taken your SATs?"

My stomach clamped on itself. I knew I should have taken them last year, but I never stepped foot back in the guidance office to find out how. I couldn't afford it anyway.

"No, I didn't get a chance," I said

"Oh, well, that's a priority. You'll need to register right away, before the deadline for the October test." She wrote a website on a sticky note and gave it to me. "There's an additional thirty-dollar fee if you register late."

My eyes fell.

"What?" she asked. "Is payment a challenge for you?"

Wow. It was like she was psychic.

"Actually, yes."

"And that's why you didn't take them last year, as well?" she asked.

I nodded.

"Have your parents considered completing an application for free and reduced lunch? If they do that, then you will be able to get fee waivers for everything else." She waited for my reply.

"Well, it's just my mom, and she never gets around to doing the paperwork for my schools." I avoided eye contact as I waited for the pity party.

"Okay, let me take care of it," she said, reaching into a stack of papers and pulling out a form. "This is an SAT fee waiver. Use this code at the bottom when filling out the online registration. You should be all set." She passed the document to me. "Let me know of anything else you need assistance with. I have my ways of helping out." She grinned and wiggled her eyebrows.

I couldn't hide my elated feelings, and a smile lit up my face. Taking the SAT was huge. It would bring me one step closer to my college dream.

"Oh, and as far as college goes," she added. "I have application fee waivers, too, and will help you navigate financial aid so we can find something perfect for you. Trust me."

My eyes lit up.

*Holy shit.*

Someone was helping me. I had no idea it was even possible to apply for college in my situation. My heart nearly burst out of my chest.

"Thank you so much, Ms. Kelly. This really means a lot to me," I gushed, nearly crying.

"Of course. That's what I'm here for," she said. Then after a brief pause, she added, "There's one thing I want you to do."

Oh, here it comes—the catch. There was always a catch.

She continued, "I want you to join my advisory group."

*Say what now?*

"What's that?" I crossed my arms.

"Every student at Lakefield is in an advisory group. It meets once a week during X-block. Students can ask questions or raise concerns and basically build connections with other students they typically wouldn't associate with. It's a community-building initiative. I think you would fit in well with my group."

*Interesting.*

Particularly since I didn't fit in well... anywhere.

"I guess," I mumbled.

"No, I insist," she said, leaving no room for negotiation. "See you third block, X block."

# CHAPTER 3

Keeping my eyes stuck to my schedule, I navigated the hallways like a champ.

The room numbers were fairly basic, all first-floor classrooms beginning with a one and second-floor starting with a two. Check. Wings A, B, C, and D—all major subjects, each with their own wing. Check. Turning into my first period class before the bell and bumping right into beautiful boy. Not check.

In my haste, I turned into my AP English class and bumped right into him as he was setting his backpack down.

"Sorry. Crap." I mumbled, shimmying past him.

"Oh, new girl," he pointed his finger at me in recognition and smiled. "Welcome to literary hell," he warned.

His smile left me temporarily blind and mute. Not knowing what to say, I kept my focus on my escape to the first available seat.

Settling in, I replayed his words in my mind. *New Girl.* Obnoxious. *Literary hell.* Okay, so this class must have a reputation of being a killer. Heads-up appreciated.

At least I had *him* to distract me from the torture.

*What? No! Head down. No contact.*

He remained turned around and his eyes stuck to me like glue but, I ignored him as best as possible.

What was his deal? Why couldn't he just ignore me? I clearly wasn't that interesting.

His attention wasn't the only thing smothering me, though. Two gorgeous girls sitting right behind him glared at me now, like they were his protective minions. Their perfect hair and make-up, and impeccable fashion sense, caused instant insecurity to poison my veins.

*Ugh. I hated that feeling!*

No matter how fake or mean I knew they were, their disapproving glares still always hit me in my self-loathing weakness.

Obviously, beautiful boy was theirs and how dare I even consider bumping into him like a moron.

Sticking to my rule-number-one, I kept my eyes down, averting all possible interaction and therefore, altercation. I needed a re-set to help me fade back into oblivion.

Picking at the dark eggplant color under my nails, I wished for the seconds to move faster. Without looking up, it was clear all eyes were on me.

*Come on, teacher. Can't you see we are ready for learning?*

*Oh my god.* My guidance counselor was right.

I put a lot of focus on my academics. Clearly, it was my shield. My escape.

Finally, the teacher came in, and all eyes turned forward, off me.

Thankfully, his bad suit and shiny bald head were distraction enough. Judging by every student's straightened spine and eyes forward, I had to assume he was a strict, no BS teacher.

"Good morning class," he stated. "I'm Mr. Benson. Welcome to AP English Literature. I'm sure you are all here on recommendation from last year's teachers." His eyes fell on me as if I didn't belong, and then he started again. "We have a lot to cover in a short amount of time and..."

Blah, blah, blah.

My mind turned to more exciting topics. All I needed from him was direction and what pages to study. I'd take care of the rest.

I was more intrigued by the protective body language of the mean girls and their eyes plastered on beautiful boy.

Okay, I had to stop calling him that. It was just wrong. But at the moment, it seemed so right.

My eyes moved around the room. In an instant, I cataloged the social standing of every student, their aspirations, and their apparent attempts at gaining favor from the it-girls and anyone else who would pay attention. Even though it was senior year, the same pathetic maneuvers were happening all around me.

The students were much like every teenager in every high school across the country—a broad mix of cultures and attitudes, skin tones and nationalities. It was very real-world here, and I liked the natural feel of it. The only difference from my previous experiences, though, was that these kids were more entitled. They flaunted all the name brands and shiny new kicks, brand new cell phones and techno-watches galore. Underneath all the privilege, though, were the same insecure, frightened adolescents. Only, with all the gadgets and glam, they had a lot to hide behind to disguise their true fears.

Then Mr. Benson's voice broke through my multiple layers of processing as he called attendance.

"Benjamin Drake."

"Here."

"Sam Frye."

"Here."

More names and I zoned out again.

Then my eyes shot wide as he called the next name.

"Dominic Murphy."

Beautiful boy lifted his hand.

"Yeah, here. Dom," he replied.

My breath stopped as I heard his name. Finally. A name.

"Elaine Rosco," Mr. Benson continued.

"Laney," pretty-girl-number-one said, flipping her perfectly straightened hair behind her shoulder and smirking.

Mr. Benson hesitated from the display, then said, "Okay. Seth Tilman."

"Here."

Mr. Benson was reaching the end of the alphabet and hadn't called my name yet. Damn it. I didn't want to have to draw any unnecessary attention to myself. What if my name wasn't on his list? What if I was in the wrong room? My heart rate accelerated, causing my face to burn. Humiliation approached and hovered just around the corner.

Mr. Benson's voice punched me in the face as he added, "And a late addition to my roster, new student, Douglas Brynn." His eyes searched the room.

I snapped to attention in horror.

*No, he did not.* He did not just call my last name first.

I shrank in my chair. Jesus Christ, Mr. Benson. Really?

I lifted my hand slightly, noting the shake in my fingers.

"Um, it's Brynn. *Brynn* Douglas," I choked.

He checked his roster once again.

"Oh, right. Sorry," he replied. "Welcome, Brynn."

His voice faded out as I caught the snickers of the pretties. I was fairly sure my new nickname was going stick, probably behind my back at first. I supposed there could be worse names than Douglas, but it was just the sheer fact that they had ammunition already. Shit. They made no attempt at hiding their chastising, and somehow, this time, it actually mattered.

Because of Dom.

Fuck.

My cardinal rule. Broken.

Everything was already falling to shit.

Second period had its own laundry list of issues.

First of all, it was AP Physics, and the teacher had a hands-off approach, assuming we were all capable of teaching ourselves. And the class mix, well, it was all the pre-med and engineering wanna-bes. At least this would be a less drama-filled class, I hoped.

"You seem really calm for just starting in a new school," the girl next to me leaned in and whispered.

Her warm brown eyes felt safe, and I shrugged one shoulder.

"I guess I like this class better than my last one," I said.

"What did you have?" she asked, pushing her long black hair behind her ear.

"Benson's AP Lit." I watched her for a reaction.

She chuckled. "Yeah, that's a ball-buster. They call him the Senior Slayer."

I huffed and nodded.

"Something tells me you'll be fine in there," she added. "No worries. It's the group of kids that'll be the pain-in-the-ass. Half of them are in it just to look good on their college apps. They know they'll fail, but by that time, they'll already have acceptance letters in hand. Just be ready."

Hmm. She seemed to know what she was talking about, and I seemed to know the exact pains-in-the-asses she was referring to.

I liked her already.

*Damn it!*

What was my problem?

I was supposed to keep my head down.

What *was* it about this school? It was almost as if a few select students jumped out at me and I couldn't help but pay attention to them. It was like they were in full clarity of my sight while all the others were a faded blur.

There was a strange, subtle heaviness around me too. Like a secret everyone knew but wouldn't talk about. It covered the entire town. Everyone and everything looked so perfect, clean, and polished, which made me wonder what they were really hiding.

I always picked up on things like that. I could sense when something was amiss. And here, in this new school, this new town, something was off.

I bit my thumbnail, pondering the unnerving feeling, then she pulled my attention back.

"Lab partner?"

"Huh?" I blinked at her.

"We need to choose lab partners," she said.

"Oh, yeah. Okay."

"I'm Poorva, by the way," she added with a smile.

"I'm Brynn."

She nodded like she already knew that and I rubbed my temples to release the tension.

The rest of the period slogged forward, and I stared at the clock which moved slower than physically possible.

Finally, at the bell, Poorva jumped up and grabbed her backpack. She slid her feet back into her Converse while keeping the heels crushed down.

"X-block," she stated. "With Ms. Kelly."

*Wait.*

Poorva was in my X-block with Ms. Kelly... and she already knew I was in there too?

I didn't know if I should be weirded-out by that or if I should just be happy.

"Come on," she said. "You're gonna love Ms. Kelly. We have the best advisory group in the school."

"Um, okay," I mumbled, trying to keep up with her quick pace.

"People kind of hate us for it," she added. "They know we have something really cool going on, but it pisses them off that they have no idea what it is." She laughed, and it sounded almost musical.

"So, I guess I'm lucky then?" My tone gave away my cynicism.

"You could say that. But it's not really a *chance* kind of thing. You're either in it or you're not." She turned down the C wing toward guidance. "Ms. Kelly chooses carefully. She's never wrong."

I slowed a bit, wondering what she was talking about.

"Chooses what?" I asked with a curled lip.

She stopped short and stared at me. Then she let out a stifled laugh.

"Oh, you don't *know*," she chuckled. "Sorry. You really *are* new. I must sound crazy." She started fast-walking again and shook her head. "Anyway, you'll see."

We flew through the hallway and noticed a couple of other students heading with similar determination in the same direction. They were clear in my vision, while all the other students in the corridor were a blur. I blinked and squinted my eyes, trying to bring the other students into focus, but it was no use. The same two were the only ones that stood out to me.

"Are they going too?" I asked Poorva.

Her jaw fell open as she glanced at the students I gestured toward.

"Uh, yuh." She stared at me for a second then pulled me along into the guidance suite.

College flags and posters lined the walls, and a row of computers ran along the far side. Several round tables filled the center of the space, and individual offices lined the perimeter.

I recognized Ms. Kelly's office door with its cheerful welcome sign. Only this time, I was coming from the other direction. The main office was down the narrow corridor past her office. I shuddered, hoping the nasty secretary had nothing to do with X-block advisory and was glad she was far out of view.

Poorva and I sat at a round table and the two other students settled at the one next to us. The boy was small, probably a freshman or sophomore, but held a look of true confidence that squashed any preconceived notions of a Napoleon Complex. The girl hid behind her long, messy hair—I mean, hasn't-been-brushed-in-a-month, messy hair.

Then, the door opened, and another student entered. He was familiar to me, and his vibrant energy pulled my attention directly to his eyes. It was the boy from the top of the stairs at the front entryway when I'd first arrived at school. He held my gaze now, again.

"Sup." He nodded at me.

I swallowed and nodded back.

"So, that's Shane," Poorva whispered. "He's a junior." Then she pointed to the others. "That's Blake, sophomore, and Courtney, junior."

The door opened again, and I watched as the next student entered.

His eyes met mine with a knowing grin.

"You following me?" Dom said, staring into my eyes.

"Um, no," I fumbled through my inner freak-out. Mute once again, I gritted my teeth at my inability to function.

Poorva came to the rescue.

"Wait, you know each other already?" she asked.

"Yeah," Dom said. "New girl. She's in my Lit class."

"You're in that class too?" Poorva groaned at him.

"Gotta get into college, ya know," he teased. "Can't get in on charm alone."

She rolled her eyes with a sigh, revealing her exasperation at students playing the system.

He pointed back at me. "I knew you'd be in here. Knew it!"

My eyebrows pulled together, and before another comment was spoken, Ms. Kelly approached us.

"Good morning group," she greeted us with a smile.

She sat at a round table as if she were one of us. Then she glanced around the space and stood again.

Looking into the conference room behind her, she said, "Come on. Let's head in there for some privacy. We have a new member as you can see, and she'll have a few questions."

I wondered why we would need the privacy of the conference room for my questions.

Everyone groaned as they pulled themselves up from the comfort of their seats, and we moved into the new space.

The conference room had a large rectangular table in the center with at least twelve chairs around it. A projector hung from the ceiling, and the whiteboard had smeared colors of erasable marker on it.

As everyone found a new seat, Ms. Kelly said, "Students, I want to introduce you to Brynn, the newest member of our group."

I dropped my eyes to my hands.

"Brynn," she said, pointing around the table. "This is Blake, Courtney, Shane, Dom, and Poorva. They will be the members of your advisory group this year, and there is much you can learn from them."

*From them?*

I was confused and was certain the twist on my face exposed that fact.

Ms. Kelly grinned. "These are the other sensitives in the school, Brynn. Like you. And it is here, in this advisory group, that you will all practice your gifts and learn to use them to their fullest."

I looked around at the others in the group, waiting for someone to burst out laughing, but no one did.

"Like a school hidden within a school," Poorva whispered.

"Huh?" I shook my head.

Ms. Kelly continued. "If you keep an open mind for the next half hour, Brynn, you'll understand what we are all about."

I stared at her, unblinking.

"We keep it hidden though," Shane blurted. "It would be social suicide to expose this."

I looked back at Ms. Kelly for her answer to his random comment.

"Yes," she said. "Our mission is delicate. The wellbeing of the community relies on us, whether they know it or not. And the last thing we need is a witch hunt on our hands. We must remain a secret academy in order to learn how to use our powers and carry out our goals."

My mind spiraled into a slushy haze.

*Secret Academy? Gifts? Witch hunt?*

I needed to switch advisory groups.

Like, now.

# CHAPTER 4

Halfway through the thirty-minute X-block, I'd heard all about astral projection, channeling, levitation, aura reading, and second sight. Ms. Kelly and the other students spoke of these things as if they were normal. Some of it reminded me of palm-readers at honky-tonk beach towns or like a scene from Dr. Strange, but other parts seemed creepy and disturbing. And these students planned to practice and use their so-called gifts and abilities like it was a competitive sport.

"So, you can see now why we keep our group a secret," Ms. Kelly said.

I nodded, unable to speak a word for fear of sounding condescending.

She added, "After hearing about the other's gifts, have you been able to connect at all with your own?"

"Huh?" I muttered.

"Do you know what *your* gift is?" she asked.

All eyes stared at me as I froze.

What was wrong with these people? They were out of their minds and didn't even know it.

All I could focus on was how to get out of the conference room and never return to this crazy advisory group.

Blake stared at me, wondering if I was about to run. Courtney looked like she saw flames. I glanced at Shane, and he watched me with a hopeful glance, wishing I would stay. Dom seemed lost within all the chaos, and Poorva held solid confidence in the belief I would accept it all.

My eyes narrowed as I processed every detail and emotion that surrounded me. I could read it all with no trouble.

How did I know so well what they were all thinking and feeling? It was the first time I'd ever actually considered it.

I *always* knew what people were thinking and feeling.

That was normal. Right?

Ms. Kelly smiled.

"The bell's going to ring in about a minute," she said.

No one moved.

They continued to stare at me, waiting.

My instinct to run coursed through my veins, tweaking my twitch muscles. But for some reason, I refused to follow my typical exit plan. Instead, I looked at each student and Ms. Kelly, and recognized a tribe around me—a group of people with common goals, to support one another, and to explore the unknown.

Maybe this was what I'd always been searching for.

Maybe this was where I belonged.

A lump formed in my throat, making it difficult to swallow.

I put my fist to my mouth and coughed.

"Um, I... I can feel your energy," I mumbled. "I... I know how you are all feeling."

Shane burst out of his seat. "Ah-ha! I knew it," he shouted, pointing at me.

Poorva's eyebrows shot up as she studied me with satisfaction.

"Clairvoyance," Blake stated with a confident nod.

My eyes widened as I allowed myself to absorb the moment.

My statement had opened a new level of honesty I'd never allowed before. I'd exposed myself, not only to these new people but to myself as well.

For years, I'd hid the truth—my true nature. And now, it hung out there in the wide-open, for all to see.

"Thank you, Brynn," Ms. Kelly stated with purpose. "And congratulations. You've just been formally inducted into our secret society."

A slight smile threatened the corners of my mouth as I glanced around the table at my new advisory group of sensitives. It was my first day at Lakefield High, and I'd just chucked my defensive plan to the wind. This could be either really good or terribly bad—there was no way to know for sure, but the twist in my gut sent warning through me. I repositioned myself in my seat to help settle it.

"Next week...," Ms. Kelly's voice broke my concentration. "We'll set our goals for the year, and I'll review the first project objectives with you."

The bell rang over her final words.

Everyone stood and grabbed their backpacks.

"Thanks, Ms. Kelly," Shane called as he jumped toward the door.

Poorva flew to my side. "What do you have now?" she asked.

Her question hovered on my brain as I continued to stare in shock at Ms. Kelly. How had she known? Somehow, they all knew. It was all so strange.

"Brynn?" Poorva poked.

"What?" I snapped my attention to her.

"What class is next?" she repeated.

*Oh. Shit.* I had no idea where I was going.

I reached into the outer pocket of my pack and pulled out the schedule Ms. Kelly had printed for me earlier. I pushed the folded paper open and scanned the grid.

"Umm..." I struggled to read it.

Poorva reached over, her long black hair falling onto the edge of it. She trailed her finger down the first column. "Okay, you have APUSH with Harrison. She's crazy," she giggled, pushing me toward the door. "It'll be mostly juniors in there, so, yeah."

I turned back to Ms. Kelly and waved to her. "Thank you," I mouthed.

She grinned, and I knew she was proud of me.

The feeling nearly burst my heart open. I don't think anyone ever felt that way about me before. She believed in me from the start and now she was excited for my journey.

And, actually, so was I.

I stumbled through the maze of tables in the guidance suite and followed Poorva out the door.

"What the hell is APUSH? I don't think I signed up for that." I studied my schedule, still lost at how to read it.

"AP US History," she laughed. "Harrison's a huge feminist. Be prepared for your ears to bleed. She has some pretty explicit stories and videos, all for shock value. Female genital mutilation is her favorite topic of discussion."

Poorva's voice faded in and out as I walked through the halls, connecting with a new part of myself with every step.

I couldn't wait until next week's X-block. I wanted to learn more about the other kids and their abilities. I'd only been half-listening at first, dismissing most of it, and now I regretted my closed mind. The group had opened it slightly, and the thrill was all-consuming.

"What did Ms. Kelly mean by 'first project'?" I asked.

"Oh, every advisory group does a few projects throughout the year, like community service stuff or fundraisers," she said. "Ours are different, though."

"Of course they are," I interrupted.

She huffed.

"Yeah, well, we make them look like community-based projects, because, in actuality, they are. But if the principal had any idea of the danger we put ourselves in, she'd flip. Ms. Kelly would probably be fired."

"Wait. Danger?" I stopped short.

"Sort of." She shrugged. "I mean, our projects typically have to do with using our psychic abilities, you know, for solving... problems."

"What kind of problems?"

"Mysteries, basically. Situations the police can't solve or reports of paranormal activity. It could be anything, really. We never know until Ms. Kelly reveals the project." She hitched her pack higher on her shoulder. "I gotta go this way." She angled to the left. "You're down there." She pointed to the history hallway. "Maybe see you at lunch," she called as she headed in the other direction.

I stared at her back as she moved away from me. I had so many more questions, it was ridiculous.

*Police matters? Paranormal activity? Danger?*

What the fuck?

I shuffled into APUSH like a distracted zombie. My mind scrambled through every detail of the past few hours. It was more information in three hours than I'd had in the previous three years of high school.

Grabbing a seat near the back, I kept my head down—finally finding a moment to return to my normal introverted behavior.

"Uh, yo, Violet," a voice nudged at me from behind. "You gonna just ignore me?"

I turned to the last row behind me and stared right into Shane's face.

"Hey," I whispered. "You're in here?"

"Duh."

I huffed. "Right. It's mostly juniors. Makes sense."

My shoulders relaxed from the perk of knowing someone in there.

"What, did you fail this class last year?" he snarked.

I turned to face front again, ignoring his jab.

"Oh, too soon?" he poked again.

"Hang on a sec," I shot back to him. "I'm having a look around for somewhere else to sit."

I wasn't really, but hell, he deserved it.

## URBAN MYSTIC ACADEMY: FIRST PROJECT

"Ooh, wounded. You got me. I'll be good now." He folded his hands nicely on his desk.

Turning again, I whispered, "Kinda funny, I had Dom in my first class, then Poorva, now you." I tipped my head.

"Yup. Ms. Kelly makes the schedules. Remember?" He wiggled his eyebrows.

Right. She probably tried to put as many of us together as possible. Made sense.

And it was perfect because I had so much I wanted to ask him. It was impossible to filter it all into one coherent question. I needed to know how each one of them got recruited, what their individual gifts were, how much control they had, but it all channeled into one point: what we would be doing together.

"So, what do you think our first project will be?" I asked under my breath.

All eyes in the room burned into my back, but it didn't bother me. I was used to being the new kid, but this time, it was actually okay. I felt like I had a squad already, and it was only day one. I didn't care if it was a motley crew of varying grade levels, styles, and basically everything else. We were different in the school, and together, we had strength. I felt the connection growing between us all now, even when we were apart.

"Don't know." He shrugged. "The new project's always a secret until the last second."

I narrowed my eyes, searching him for more information. He was a tough read.

"Well, what was the last one?" I pressed.

"No can tell. We're sworn to secrecy with anyone who wasn't a part of it." He gave an eavesdropper the stink-eye. "I can tell you it was a doozy, though. Nearly lost my shit more than once."

My eyes widened.

What the hell was Ms. Kelly sending these kids to do? And why was she willing to put her job on the line for it?

"Eyes on me, please," a sharp voice cut through the room.

I twisted front immediately and watched Ms. Harrison survey the room. She pegged a couple guys with her glare, making assumptions that they would be the challenging ones and that she would put them in their places, likely by humiliation.

Oof. She was a tough one. It was like she'd had a rough life and this was her opportunity to right the wrongs of the past. Payback, really.

She nodded slightly when she glanced at me. She liked my hair. Thought it was a powerful statement and wondered if I was psychologically damaged.

*Whoah.* I was doing it.

I understood everything that was going through her mind and everything she felt.

I'd always done it. But now, I realized it wasn't something everyone could do. It was my *gift*. And apparently, I still had a lot to learn about how to use it.

But it could be dangerous.

Shane made that clear.

And so did Poorva.

Did I really want to tap into this further and open the potential for getting hurt? The concept was directly against my principles of self-preservation.

*Don't make bonds with anyone, or you get hurt.*

*Don't get involved in something that matters, or you get hurt.*

*Don't rely on anyone but yourself, or you get hurt.*

I was sick of getting hurt.

I'd had a lifetime of instability and broken friendships. Remaining detached was my best defense.

But now, I was being offered something enormous. Something that I'd been dreaming of my entire life but hadn't even realized it.

Should I take it or should I turn my back on it?

I had really just wanted to lay low here for a quiet senior year. But now, with all of this, I would become more than a shadow in the hallways.

My inner debate grated my teeth together, like two sides of me duking it out—the good angel of one shoulder and the evil devil on the other.

But the winner was clear.

I'd decided a long time ago, and now, I was at the point of no return.

I'd been initiated into the secret academy, and I vowed to give it everything I had.

The devil had won.

# CHAPTER 5

While walking home, there was a slight lift in my step. The second half of the school day had been a blur, surviving the drone of boring teachers and glaring students, but it didn't matter. My mind swam with far more than calculus and lunchroom drama. I had something special, and I was dying to learn more about it.

I flipped through all my memories in my mind—all the times I'd felt sensations around me, more than I should have, and understanding things that others were unaware of. The memories flooded me. All these years, I'd thought I was overly sensitive or vulnerable when actually, I was super-aware of the subtle energies that surrounded me.

Excitement oozed from every nerve as I stepped up my front stoop. Our home was a small in-law apartment at the side of someone's beautiful house. Apparently, the mother-in-law had moved to an assisted-living facility, leaving the space vacant. Little did the owner know, my mother was unreliable in the department of paying rent, but our assistance program probably made us look stellar.

I pushed the door open with a gentle exhale. It felt like I'd been lost for years and suddenly found the right path.

I was home.

"The bathroom still looks like shit." My mother's voice slapped me in the face. "And you look ridiculous. Again. No one's going to talk to you at school with hair like that. You might as well be wearing a 'keep away from the crazy girl' sign." She dropped her head back on the couch.

My chest caved in from her hurtful attack. The muscles around my heart constricted, as usual, and my shoulders curled in. How did her words hold so much power to hurt me?

"It's not that unusual to have hair color like this," I replied. "I mean, it's bold, sure, but it's not crazy."

I didn't know why I felt it necessary to defend my hair. It was part of who I was, my armor, and it was here to stay.

"It makes you look cheap," she mumbled.

I shrugged. She always said that about everything I did. It was probably what she had heard all her young life. I decided to deflect her negativity and change the subject.

"Any word from the temp agency?" I asked, hopeful that maybe she had a job opportunity lining up.

"Nah, I'm gonna check out the DPW tomorrow. I saw a sign out front when I walked to the convenient store. Says they're hiring."

"Oh, that sounds good." I allowed a glimmer of hope to enter my soul.

"Yeah, well, we'll see. If nothing turns up, we'll just head to the next town." She grabbed the remote and flicked to the local news channel.

I never knew why she watched the local news. The headlines were always tragedies like house fires and shootings, and this time it was about two missing children. I cringed and turned away from it.

A moment later, I gasped for air.

I hadn't realized I'd stopped breathing.

Her casual mention of moving to another town had been like a sucker-punch to the gut, knocking my wind out. I didn't want to move towns again. I liked my new school, and I had made some friends already.

*Argh!* This was precisely why I should have kept my head down.

But, no. It was too late.

I would fight to stay this time.
I was almost eighteen, and if I had to stay on my own, I would.
I counted the weeks on my fingers until my birthday.
Ten.
I prayed it would be enough time.

I'd spent the rest of the week scouring, not only purple stains in the bathroom but also websites on psychics and paranormal things. Some of it was useful, and some just freaked me out. I was left with more questions than answers.

Friday had crept up on me faster than it ever had, and while rolling out of bed, I was actually disappointed. The coming weekend would be slow and tedious while waiting for Monday's arrival.

*Shit.* This was the first time I'd ever wished away a Friday and hoped for a Monday, but getting back to the advisory block was my primary focus.

Pulling on my favorite jeans and t-shirt, I prepped myself for the day and checked my reflection. The pink color in my cheeks and bright blue eyes shocked me. I looked good. I grabbed my mascara off the bureau and added some to the tips of my lashes, then flew out the door.

Rushing to school, I thought through all the assignments I'd neglected the night before. I'd have to use every free moment this morning to catch up, and surprised myself for having been so distracted. I bolted into AP Lit just as the bell rang and fell into my seat, breathless.

Dom turned and sent me a grin. I smiled back quickly, but just as the split-second exchange occurred, Laney shot a glare my way. Instantly, she bent into her friend's ear and whispered while keeping one eye pegged on me.

*What was her deal?* She didn't even know me, and she'd already targeted me.

I focused on Mr. Benson as he finished taking attendance, then got lost in his immediate drone about Great Expectations.

My mind wandered through the numerous things I wanted to research further, including mind-reading and clairvoyance, and I wished for time to pass faster. Before I knew it, the bell snapped me back to reality, and I shot out of my seat by instinct.

As I lifted my backpack and swung it over my shoulder, it hit off something solid and bounced back at me. I turned in surprise and stared into Dom's handsome face. His dark hair and ultra-thick eyebrows framed his deep blue eyes perfectly, and his grin activated a dimple that weakened my knees.

"Whoa, careful with that thing," he joked. "You could hurt somebody."

"Sorry," I gasped. "I didn't see you there."

"Ouch." He reached for his heart like I'd hurt his feelings. "No, really, it's okay."

His dimple taunted me, and I pulled my eyes away, only to land directly on Laney, waiting by the door, staring at us.

"Physics next," I said, taking a step away. The last thing I needed was drama with Laney.

"Yeah, I'm going that way too," he said, following my lead.

I hesitated for a second, fairly certain his next class was in the other direction. He'd gone that way every other day this week.

I hoisted my pack higher on my shoulder and shimmied past Laney. She didn't move an inch to allow me easier passage, but I pushed through either way. As soon as I was past her, though, she blocked Dom's way entirely and stopped him.

"Any big plans for the weekend?" she purred into his neck. "You won't want to miss the bonfire at Sammy's." She spoke loud enough for me to hear.

He pressed her away from his personal space and said, "Don't know yet. I'm sure I'll figure something out." He tried to step past her to catch up to me, but she sidestepped in his way again.

"Text me," she whispered, turning to me to be sure I was watching.

She caught my eyes, and my face reddened. I wasn't sure if it was embarrassment for being caught staring or if it was anger from her derailing my moment with Dom. Either one was humiliating, and I turned and jetted for my physics class.

Without looking back, I barreled down the hall into the science classroom and thumped down next to Poorva. My sigh could be heard for miles.

"Okay, what'd I miss?" she gushed.

I smiled, loving her intrigue of gossip and all-things-dramatic.

"Laney again," I hissed.

"Figures." She rolled her eyes. "What's she up to now?"

I paused for a second, careful about my next words so it wouldn't sound like I was hot for Dom or anything. But no matter how I rephrased the last moments in my head, it made me sound like I was hot for Dom.

*Shit.* Maybe I was.

"She interferes with everything I try to do. You know. She's targeted me, and harassing me is like sport to her." I pulled my notebook out and splatted it on my desk.

"Dom, right?"

"Hmm?" I avoided eye contact.

"Dom. She thinks she owns him," she stated. "She can see he's interested in you, and she can't stand it." She chuckled.

*Interested in me?* I paused on the idea and batted the butterflies down in my stomach.

"You know, you guys are in the academy together, of course he's going to be intrigued with you," she added.

*Oh. Right.* We were in the secret academy together, so obviously he'd want to know more about me. Made sense. I had to stop letting my imagination run away with itself.

"Yeah, well, Laney's obnoxious and needs to get over herself," I huffed.

"Too true. You're not the first she's tried to make untouchable." She shook her head.

"What does that mean?"

"You know," she said. "She says shit to get people to think someone's cringy and then if someone else is seen talking to them, they'll be outcasted as well. It's a huge power move by the queen bee. Keeps all her little worker bees in check."

Sounded childish, but unfortunately it also sounded very effective.

"I don't give a shit." I opened my notebook. "Let her. It wouldn't be the first time," I murmured.

It was so unfair, though. I didn't even have a chance for people to get to know me before Laney's plans to end me were put into motion. Once I was untouchable, no one would be able to approach me, or apparently their social status would be compromised. It sickened me. We were about to launch into the world as adults, and still, they all played these immature games.

What was worse, though, was the fact that the games bothered me so much.

Surviving physics, and then APUSH, brought me to the point in the day that every high-schooler dreaded. Lunch.

Walking into the cafeteria was the most horrifying part of the day. A sea of faces and endless chatter filled the void-of-despair, and I searched for a place to sit, while at the same time, trying to look confident and not lost. It sucked shit.

I walked past the round tables and moved by the long, narrow ones, cursing the fact that I'd allowed Shane to bound away after APUSH. I supposed it would be awkward to sit with juniors anyway.

Then my attention snapped over my shoulder.

"Hey, Douglas." Her voice scratched my ears like the squeak of cutting Styrofoam.

My eyes narrowed, and I glared at Laney. Her minions around her stared back at me, protecting their queen bee.

"Isn't this funny," she said, holding her phone out at me. A random picture lit up on her screen and looked like an old yogi guru man in traditional Indian clothes. By instinct, I squinted to see the pic better and fake-smirked while continuing my search for a seat. "It looks like Poorva. Right?" She laughed.

As soon as I heard Poorva's name, I glared back at her and grimaced in disgust.

*What the fuck? What an idiot.*

And what did she have against Poorva?

Oh, right. Poorva was gorgeous, and Laney knew we were becoming friends. That made Poorva a target as well, I figured.

*Great.*

There goes my first friend.

I kept walking until I reached the exit and sat outside the caf in the lobby.

Alone.

Welcome to high school hell, I thought and nibbled on my dry peanut butter sandwich while staring at my phone.

"Room for two?" A voice broke me out of my isolation prison.

I looked up and stared into Shane's friendly face.

He sat next to me on the bench, flipping his hair from his eyes, and pulled out his bag lunch. "The caf sucks for new kids," he said, unwrapping his turkey sandwich—clearly made by a loving mother, tomatoes and mayo to boot. "Sucks for everyone, actually, so don't feel bad. They're all faking it in there anyway. Some better than others. But no one's actually comfortable."

I huffed. "Yeah, you're probably right."

"Oh, I know I'm right. Trust me." He smirked.

I nodded, assuming he was referring to his gift. He probably had more information than I'd realized. Maybe even about me too.

"Don't let them get to you," he added. "Just see them as an extra hurdle to get past each day, in order to be able to practice in the academy."

I took a big bite of my sandwich. "You're right. That's helpful. Thanks," I mumbled through my full mouth.

He chuckled and took a big bite of his sandwich too.

"Did you hear they found those missing kids?" He glanced through the lobby to be sure no one was listening.

"Wait, those two boys?" I asked, remembering the local news story in the back of my mind.

"Yeah. It's weird, right?" He shook his head. "This town has some bizarre secrets it's hiding. Like, it's not the first time kids have gone missing in those woods. And they have no memory of what happened when they're found. Freakyyyyy."

"Are you serious? That's creepy." I stopped chewing and stared at him.

"I know. Makes you rethink a camping trip, right?" he said.

I grinned. He lightened my mood, and I liked the way he sat next to me with such comfort, knees splayed out in his athletic pants, and his worn vintage T hanging loose at the waist.

His thin build worked for him, like a soccer player, and made the lean muscles in his arms more defined. I took a quick second to notice his attractive face and wondered why more girls weren't hanging around him. His longish light brown hair added a playful element to his casual look and completed it perfectly. The narrow-minded junior girls had no idea what they were missing.

"I hate the woods anyway, so I'll stay safe right here in civilization, thank you very much," I joked.

"What? You don't like hiking?" His light blue eyes burst wide in astonishment. "Hiking's the best."

I thought for a moment about my past hiking experiences—poison ivy, biting flies, garter snake attack when trying to pee discretely. Ummm, no. I'm good.

"Not much," I said. "It's not for me."

"Hmm. Well, maybe you just haven't been on the right hike. You know." He bumped his knee into mine and took another bite of his sandwich.

"Yeah," I shrugged, biting mine too. "Maybe."

# CHAPTER 6

How could a mere half-hour hold so much power?

It felt like I'd been waiting centuries for the next X-block to roll around, and it was finally here. I'd done enough research over the weekend on extrasensory perception and clairvoyance to last a lifetime, and had the bonus of learning about all the sub-categories as well. Like things out of a witchcraft movie, I never considered these abilities could actually be real.

But now, I was a true believer.

There was something bigger around us that most people didn't perceive.

I'd felt it all my life. And now, I was ready to unleash it.

And I was more than ready now for Ms. Kelly's big reveal about our first project.

The walk to school had been a blur, and once I was in the halls of Lakefield High, I searched for Poorva. We usually bumped into each other in the hangout area in front of the library doors. There was no sign of her this morning, so I sulked off to first period.

"Ignoring my follow request?" Dom's voice broke me out of my sullen mood.

"What? No," I stuttered, shooting him a puzzled look.

I grabbed my phone on instinct and looked at it.

He raised his eyebrows in judgment.

"My wifi sucks," I said. "And honestly, I don't check my social media apps very often. My notifications are off." I swiped around on my apps and accepted his request with a guilty grin.

"Hey, Douglas," Laney chimed in. "Got your first follower?"

I ignored her and moved to my seat.

Two seconds later, my phone buzzed. I glanced at it through narrow eyes, then smirked. Dom had sent me a message.

It was a pic of his desk with the words *'xblock today'* typed across the screen.

So, I wasn't alone in my eager anticipation. It was funny that he was just as excited as I was, and I counted the minutes like they were an eternity.

As soon as the bell rang, I bolted to physics. I could tell Dom was lingering by his desk, waiting for a chance to talk again, but with Laney there messing things up, I kept my head down and left. I didn't want to let her win so easily, but I also didn't want to deal with her petty comments and constant jabbing.

I'd have my chance to see Dom later in X-block.

Without her.

A guilty twang hit my stomach as I wished the advisory period was more than thirty minutes.

Barreling into physics, I locked my eyes on Poorva, and darted over to her. Dropping into my seat with a huff, I waited for her to look at me, but she didn't move.

"Hey, what's up?" I said.

She glanced over and shrugged.

It wasn't her usual greeting, full of intrigue to hear the latest gossip from AP Lit.

Something was wrong.

She'd never acted cold like this before, and it was clear she was unhappy.

"Okayyy...," I pressed. "What's going on? Did I do something?"

She dropped her shoulders and exhaled. "Ever hear of betrayal?"

she snapped.

"What?" I choked.

"You think it's funny that I look like an old Indian man?"

I pulled back in confusion. "What the hell are you talking about?"

She grabbed her phone and flashed a photo at me. It looked familiar, but I wasn't sure why.

"Laney posted it on her story," she said. "And all her minions commented that you thought it was funny. That's humiliating, Brynn." She pulled her phone back.

I froze in confusion. I'd fallen victim to the classic set-up.

"Shit, Poorva. You have to know that's not true. I had no idea what that picture was when she flashed it at me in the caf. I swear." I stared at her, waiting for a response. "You have to know she's only trying to mess things up between us."

I sensed she believed me, but she was still crushed. The embarrassment was too much for her, knowing the entire school followed Laney.

My heart sank.

I had been so excited for X-block, but now, with Poorva mad at me, I couldn't think of anything else.

"Whatever," she murmured.

*Fuck.* Having Laney mess things up with Dom and me was one thing, but going after Poorva was quite another.

Poorva's insecurity about her looks oozed from her now, and I couldn't believe it. She had no idea how beautiful she was. Her dark complexion, deep brown eyes, and long, silky black hair made her look like an exotic queen. Of course, in this school, if you didn't look like Laney, then you were made to feel like a fail. Somehow, the Barbie look was still a thing.

The period dragged on like being trapped in limbo. I needed to patch things up with Poorva but, there was no chance during the tedious lecture on acceleration.

As soon as the bell rang, I hopped up and grabbed onto her arm. Locking elbows, I pulled her out of the room, leaving her no other options.

Once we were on our way toward the guidance suite, I set her free from my lock, and she kept pace with me.

"So, you know I'd never do that, right? You know I've got your back," I said. "Their approval means nothing to me. They have nothing that I want. Cool?" I slowed, waiting for her reply.

She nodded her head slowly. "Yeah, I know," she finally said. "She just knows exactly how to hit where it hurts." Her eyes fell.

"Okay, yes," I agreed. "She's very good at what she does. Power through intimidation and humiliation. We just have to fight against it. Like, don't give her the satisfaction."

She nodded. "Yup. You're right." She gave a weak smile.

I smiled back, knowing I was winning her back.

"I'm sorry that pic was sent around, though. That sucks," I added.

We turned toward guidance and bumped into Shane and Blake. The lift in their steps proved they were eager to get to X-block as well. Excitement returned to my nerves, and I jittered with anticipation.

Dom hurried in behind us with the energy of a wild horse, followed by Courtney, who kept her face hidden behind her rats-nest of hair.

As soon as the six of us gathered together, my sight brightened, and everything took on sharper clarity. A vibrating hum shot through my body, and I stared at everyone, wondering if they felt it too. Shane chuckled at me, and then Ms. Kelly came over to us.

"Morning," she welcomed us. "I've been counting the minutes. Who's ready to hear about our first project?"

Without another word, we got up and moved into the conference room and closed the door behind us. Within two seconds, we were seated and silent, staring at Ms. Kelly for her next words.

"I can see you're just as eager as I am," she started. "And I'm delighted to see you back, Brynn. We can never be too sure how well new recruits will react once they hear what we are all about."

"Oh, we know how they'll react," Shane jested. "We'd never risk it, otherwise."

Ms. Kelly smirked. "True. For the most part. But you have to remember, we never really know what each of us is capable of until we tap into it, so we can't get too confident that we truly know what's going on around us."

Blake nodded. "Yeah, like when I first joined. You guys all thought I was just a nerd." He straightened his pile of textbooks in front of him.

"No shit," Dom huffed. "But then you kicked all our asses in last year's first project. As a freshman, none the less."

"Language," Ms. Kelly reminded Dom.

"Sorry." He dropped his gaze to the table, but his dimple exposed the fact that he was smiling.

"So, I'm looking forward to practicing our exercises, but first, I thought you'd like to hear the project details."

Everyone shifted in their seats and sat taller, waiting on whatever she would say next.

She cleared her throat and began in a hushed tone. "You've all felt it in some shape or form, but maybe haven't been sure of the source. But I can assure you, there's been a re-awakening. Like a portal's been opened, allowing the demons back into our community."

My breath stopped, and I stared at her.

She scanned the room. "The two young boys who went missing in the woods, they've been found. But, like the others, they have no memory of what occurred while they were lost. The town knows it's not the first time this has happened. And it won't be the last until the mystery is solved."

Courtney dropped her head and banged it on the table.

Ms. Kelly didn't flinch at the thud and continued. "The police have brought in specialists, but I can assure you, they'll find no trace of foul play. The events are of a different realm. One they don't understand. One they can't fathom." She took a deep breath. "Our first project, my students, will be to study the local urban legend...."

Shane blurted, "Hell's Gates."

She nodded. "Gain insight into the legend of Hell's Gates, then, explore the town woods to uncover whatever it is that's been going on in our community for over three hundred years. And report your findings back to me."

My chin dropped down as I stared at her in disbelief.

Was she nuts?

That project was too big. And it sounded dangerous. And scary.

I gasped, realizing I hadn't taken a breath since she began speaking.

All eyes turned to me, and they let out nervous giggles.

"So, yeah," Shane said to me. "Welcome to the club."

Second-guessing my status as a newly initiated member of the secret-society-of-whatevers, I fidgeted in my seat, wondering if it was too late to bail.

I hated the woods.

I hated creepy legends. They kept me up at night.

And most of all, I hated words like 'open portal' and 'demons'.

I was clearly over my head.

My hand lifted on its own will, and Ms. Kelly called on me.

"Brynn. Question?" she asked.

"Umm." My mind went blank.

I had so many questions, so many excuses as to why we shouldn't get involved. My mind raced with a million options at my escape attempt. But then, something shifted within me—a curiosity that I couldn't squash. A glimpse into the supernatural world was offered to me on a platter, and there was no way I could turn my back on it.

"Well, I guess I'm just wondering," I began again. "Why us?"

She smiled, and I sensed a wave of relief wash through her as if she had expected me to quit right on the spot.

"Good question, Brynn." She glanced around the room. "You are all juveniles in the development of your abilities. That makes you hyper-sensitive and open to new experiences. This means that the six of you combined can be more powerful than any highly-experienced sensitives."

Blake chimed in. "It still sounds like something the police should be able to solve."

"You would think so," Ms. Kelly agreed. "But some of us, from my ancient order, believe there's more to it. We're sensing a supernatural current disturbing the balance around us. Our vision is shrouded, though, by thick smoke. The elders believe it's the perfect opportunity for our students, unbiased sensitives, to explore and practice their extrasensory abilities. Therefore, your first project has been established."

"Sounds cool," Shane interjected. "We've all heard of that urban legend our entire lives. It used to keep me up at night, terrified I'd be pulled into the woods, never to return." He huffed.

"Same," Dom added. "I've never actually entered those woods. Like, you were crazy to even consider it."

Courtney thumped her head on the table again, and this time, let out a small whimper.

Poorva glanced at her with concern, then said, "The legend of Hell's Gates is just a story made up to keep kids from wandering into the woods and getting lost. It seems to have worked, considering you guys believed it to some level." She smirked at the guys, then shrugged. "I don't understand why it's such a big deal now."

Ms. Kelly nodded. "There is always a hint of truth within legend, and it will be our mission to discover what that is."

Her focus moved to Courtney, who left her face hidden on the table.

It was bizarre that everyone accepted her behavior as normal, and I was ready to find out what the hell was wrong with her.

Poorva leaned closer to me. "She always does this when she hears the new project. It's like it causes emotional overload. Don't worry about it."

I stared unblinking at Poorva and then back at Courtney.

Then, without warning, Courtney shot her head up from the table and scanned the room, death-staring at each of us. Her eyes blazed with flames deep within her pupils, and she bared her teeth in a grimace of excruciating pain. Her hands gripped the edge of the table in a white-knuckled clamp, and she shuddered in her seat.

"What's wrong with her?" I blasted.

Ms. Kelly jumped up, knocking her seat to the floor, and raced to Courtney's side. She reached for her face and stared straight into her eyes.

The rest of us moved closer to see what we could do to help.

"Courtney, look at me," Ms. Kelly said with a soothing voice. "Keep control. Steady."

What the hell was happening? It was like she was having a seizure, only worse. She was being burned from the inside out.

Ms. Kelly held her gaze without flinching. "Now release it," she commanded.

Courtney let out a loud gasp, and pushed herself away from the table, panting. She dropped her head back and her hair fell away from her face.

It was my first time seeing her full features, and I was shocked at how attractive she was. Her pain had caused her face to twist and gnarl, and then with her ratty hair all over it, she initially appeared witch-like. But in fact, now I could see her natural beauty behind it all and my jaw dropped.

She gasped for air, then pulled herself upright again.

"They're still burning," she whispered. A tear fell down her cheek and she swiped at it.

Ms. Kelly nodded with understanding. "Okay, Courtney. We'll try to help. Maybe this will be the time."

My eyes shot wide, and I glanced at Poorva. Her gaze remained fixed on Ms. Kelley and Courtney. I turned to Shane and then Dom but they continued to stare at them as well.

Then I focused on Blake. He sat with his hands folded in front of him as if nothing crazy had gone on at all.

As I looked at him, a new sense of calm washed over me, and my shoulders relaxed. My teeth unclenched from their vice grip, and the aching twist in my gut released.

It would be okay. This was a normal part of our practice. Everyone's gifts manifested in different ways, and some could appear frightening at times.

The ideas soothed me as I allowed the tension to flow out of my muscles.

I blinked and stared at Blake deeper. He smiled gently and gave me a nod.

*How the hell did he do that?*

I shifted in my seat, trying to keep my cool, but my mind raced along without me, trying to make sense of what was happening.

Shit just got real. Real fast.

# CHAPTER 7

The bell rang, and I was left gasping.

X-block had ended, and I was feeling drained and frightened.

Courtney had had some kind of epic meltdown. Blake got into my head, manipulating my thoughts without saying a word. And Ms. Kelly gave us the specific instructions for our first project, and it all scared the crap out of me.

We trailed out of the conference room in silence, each one affected in their own way.

Ms. Kelly stayed back with Courtney for a moment, and I was relieved. Courtney did not seem ready to walk into her next class after nearly bursting into flames right before our eyes. And come to think of it, she never seemed ready to go to class. Her condition plagued her twenty-four seven, making it practically impossible for her to function.

"Want to be the first to go into the woods?" Dom whispered, causing me to flinch.

My mind hadn't had the chance to even consider the idea of exploring the woods. I was too distracted by the insane events that had just occurred. I really needed to roll with these concepts better if I was going to keep up.

I hesitated, considering his idea of being the first to the woods. I initially figured we'd all do some research first and discuss our approach, but it seemed like he was turning it into a race.

Maybe it *was* one.

"Don't rush her, asshole," Shane jabbed. "She's new. Remember?"

Poorva put her arm around my shoulder as if claiming me and brushed the guys away. "Back off, wolves," she laughed.

Then Ms. Kelly called to us from the conference room. "Oh, one more thing," she said.

We all froze before taking another step.

"The project will be broken into two teams," she stated.

"What?" Shane blasted, staring at her with an open mouth.

"Blake, Shane, and Poorva for the first team. Courtney, Dom, and Brynn for team two. The team approach will keep a healthy level of competition while also allowing for different strategies and skills to develop within the project." She waved her hand. "Off to class now."

We filed out of the guidance suite, already checking our calendars for the next advisory meeting. It was clear I wasn't' the only one with a load of questions.

"Teams? What the hell?" Shane complained as we moved down the hall. "I hate getting competitive with you guys."

"You just don't like your team," Dom teased. "You're such a little bitch."

"Fuck you," Shane murmured as he turned away from us and shot down the B wing.

I hurried and caught up with him as we walked toward our history class. "Wait up," I said. "What? You don't want to be seen with me?" I jabbed.

He slowed his pace. "Sorry. I'm just pissed."

"Why? Teams kinda make sense. I can see why she wants to do it that way," I said.

In honesty, I was perplexed as well. Sticking together seemed the safest approach, but I figured she knew what she was doing. As our mentor, Ms. Kelly's goal was to hone our skills as best as possible. Breaking us into groups would probably help to do that.

Shane kept his head down, avoiding eye contact. "Yup."

We moved closer to our classroom, and I wished we had more time to process our advisory meeting. Getting together with my team was a priority now, so we could plan out our next moves for the project.

"Have you ever been in those woods?" I asked him.

Shane stopped for a second and looked at me.

"Yeah. Couple times." His face grew somber. "Once on a dare. Few years ago, some of the guys in my grade, you know. I didn't want to look like a chicken-shit, so I pretended I wasn't scared and went in. Just far enough, where they couldn't see me anymore." He pressed his lips together. "Yeah, not looking forward to going back there."

"Are you serious?" My eyes widened, wondering what happened to him.

"We don't have all day," Ms. Harrison's voice pierced through my skull. "Are you waiting for an invitation?" She stood at her door, ushering us in.

I thought more about the idea of breaking into teams. My group made me nervous with just Dom and Courtney. I wasn't sure how I would navigate it, especially with Courtney's bizarre episodes. Something was clearly very wrong with that girl.

"Shane," I whispered, as we filed to the back of the room.

He stopped at our seats. "Yeah?"

"Courtney's in my group," I murmured, unable to hide my concern.

He huffed. "Yeah. You're fucked."

The first thing I did after school was create a group chat with the six of us. Poorva helped me get everyone's number, and I saved them all to my contacts.

Dom was the first to reply.

*So u do use social media*

Shane named the group, *UMA*.

Courtney remained silent, so I wasn't even sure if she used her phone or not.

Blake sent a bunch of enthusiastic emojis.

Then, before the group even had a chance to explode with questions and comments, Dom created a second group chat. This one was just Courtney, him, and me, and he named it *Champions*. His first text gave rule number one.

*Keep our strategies private in this chat*

So, the competition began.

I didn't reply to his team chat and kept my comments to the bigger group. In my mind, we were all still one big team. I hoped.

My questions flooded out of me while I simultaneously researched urban legends and the woods of Lakefield, Massachusetts. It was my first time living in the north shore of Mass, and I wasn't sure what it might be known for. Of course, the only information that popped up referred back to the nearby historic town of Salem and its witch trials. It stole all the headlines from any other cities around it. No wonder.

With nothing of interest coming up for Lakefield, I texted UMA.

*Why is there no info on the children who get lost in the woods*

Shane's ellipses showed up immediately as he typed.

*Not considered newsworthy always a coverup*

I supposed since the children were found unharmed, the stories didn't capture much attention. People craved horror stories of loss and despair on the news, so happy endings got buried.

Poorva added a line.

*Everyone in town is afraid*

Afraid of what? Bad press? A drop in real estate value?

I typed again with my question.

*Afraid of the woods*

Shane replied quickly.

*Afraid of making it angry*

He typed again.

*They think if they ignore it then it won't get worse*

My questions grew tenfold. I couldn't handle waiting another minute to figure out how we were going to approach this project. I typed.

*Screw this lets meet there tonight*
Shane typed.
*What the fuck for*
I replied.
*Planning purposes*

A few more messages flew around, and we decided to meet there at seven o'clock. My giddiness nearly bounced me out of my shoes.

As the time grew nearer, Dom had entered the chat and agreed to meet with us. Blake replied, too, saying his parents wouldn't let him out, that he had to focus on his homework. Courtney never replied.

Poorva planned to pick me up on her way there. At first, I was embarrassed to give her my address. It was obvious she came from a well-to-do family, her dad being the town attorney, and I wanted her to think the same of me. And I'd die if she met my mother. The longer I could keep Mom a secret, the better. I just didn't want to deal with having to explain those awkward dynamics right now.

For the first time in my life, I was creating my own identity, without my mother's gruff involvement—offending people without hesitation. I just wanted to forge my own path now, and not be judged for being something I wasn't. Keeping Mom hidden from Poorva was the first step in the process.

Creating my own identity was actually a little exciting. Liberating. A sense of empowerment had crept in over the last week, and I liked it. I'd always felt like a victim, being dragged around against my will, from place to place. But now, it was different. I wanted to stay here and made a silent vow to myself that I would.

My phone lit up as I was getting ready.

Dom's name popped up.

*Need a ride*

My eyes widened as I stared at the phone, and my heart raced for a second. It was dumb. He was just checking if I needed a ride, but still. I hated my girly reaction to it.

I typed back.

*All set. Poorva's getting me*
He replied.
*K*

I stared at his response, wondering what it meant. Was he mad? Disappointed? Didn't care?

Then I rolled my eyes, wanting to choke myself for being so petty.

*Ugh.* I hated this feeling.

But, okay, I loved it, too.

Before long, Poorva pulled up, and I sprang to the door before she had a chance to get out of her car.

I'd told my mother we were getting together to do homework, and she shrugged.

It was true, though. I'd just kept the intriguing details of the project to myself to avoid any additional questioning or unnecessary flexing on my freedom.

I hopped into Poorva's car, assuming it must have been one of her parent's at some point. The four-door sedan seemed more of a match for a businessman than a teenager, but either way, it was luxurious in my eyes—leather seats and a fancy chime to remind me to put my seatbelt on.

"I love your car," I gushed, spreading my hands along the sides of my seat.

"Thanks," she said. "It was my dad's. He swore about its safety features and a strong metal frame. Makes me feel like a soccer mom."

"Well, I think it's pretty. And it beats walking any day," I said, reminding my inner-self to follow up on a job at the cafe. "So, which way?"

I looked up the road, curious about which direction we would go to find our meeting location at the woods. Poorva seemed to know the spot Shane had texted about, so, I went with her lead.

"I think Shane's pretty freaked out about the project," Poorva said, driving in the direction of school. "He likes to act all cool and tough, but honestly, I think he hates this stuff."

I turned to her in surprise. "Seriously?" I considered him for a second. "I thought he loved hiking and the outdoors. Figured he'd like this." But then I remembered his story of going into those woods once on a dare, and never wanting to return. "Actually," I added. "You might be right. He did seem a little hesitant, maybe."

"Right?" she said, turning past the school.

As we moved beyond the student lot and School Crossing signs, the houses spread out farther, creating a more rural feel. The trees grew denser, and I knew we'd come to the outer edge of the town forest.

"There's a small lot up a bit farther. It has a trail map and benches. People like to walk their dogs and mountain bike there." Poorva kept an eye out for the turn.

"Don't they know about the ghost stories?" I asked.

"Yeah, they know. The stories are told to keep the kids out. And I guess everyone believes that if you leave before dusk, you'll be fine." She slowed the car, eyeballing the side of the road. "There it is."

She pulled into the turn-off, and the car bounced over rocks and dips in the dirt road. The space opened up enough to allow several cars to park, and two vehicles were already there.

A blue RAV4 and a black Jeep Wrangler.

If I had my guess, I knew exactly whose was whose. Shane got his mom's hand-me-down, and Dom had the rugged new whip.

As Poorva pulled the car in, the guys hopped out of theirs. I thought it was odd that they had remained in their vehicles until we arrived, but, maybe they'd just gotten there, too.

Once she parked, we jumped out and joined them at the benches.

Before we had the chance to sit, the sound of a roosting bird, maybe a turkey, echoed out of the woods. It caused all our heads to jerk in its direction and then Dom let out a nervous laugh.

"We're jumpy already," he teased.

"Sounds like the call of the local witch," Shane joked. "Welcoming us to her hell house."

I examined the edge of the woods for any movement and then gazed into the dark trail opening. My stomach clamped tight, sending a clear warning to my head.

I held my breath, cursing the fact that I'd suggested we come here. It was creepier than I'd expected, and I wished I was home in my bed instead. Watching the fidgeting discomfort of the others, I sensed they were feeling the same way.

Tension continued to mount as we listened to every rustle of leaves or snapping of twigs. Our silence amplified the sounds of the night-time woods to full height.

"Okay," Shane prodded in a hushed tone. "Whose idea was this?"

I shrank into my jacket.

My over-enthusiasm had a history of placing me in some pretty volatile situations. And judging by my heart pounding in my ears, this was proving to be an unsettling one.

# CHAPTER 8

Planted on the benches by the edge of the woods, we continued to stare into the trail opening, waiting for a crooked-over witch to creep out and devour us.

"It feels like we're cheating on the rest of our group," I said, trying to refocus us. "I feel bad that Blake and Courtney aren't here."

"That sounds like a *them* problem," Dom said. "We can't always wait for everyone to be able to do stuff."

I guessed he was right, but it still felt weird. Especially since this was our first official meeting, outside of school.

"We'll just have to keep them in the loop in the group chat," Poorva said, reaching for her phone. "That way, they can chime in if they want to."

"FaceTime, too," Shane added.

"Yeah, okay," I agreed.

It all sounded like a decent compromise. I figured if worse came to worst, and *I* was the one who couldn't attend, I'd be okay with FaceTime—as long as I was still a part of the action in some way.

Poorva typed into the group chat.

"So, why are we here?" Shane aimed his pointed question at me while keeping an eye over his shoulder at the dark opening to the woods.

I fidgeted for a second, unsure of how to respond, wondering if I was wasting everyone's time. I just couldn't help it, though. I was curious about absolutely everything and couldn't stand to lose a single opportunity to explore.

"I think it's a good idea for us to plan together. Like, I have a ton of questions about this place and well, this group." I looked at each of them, reminding with my lost gaze that this was all new to me. "I just need to know what the hell is going on."

Dom let out a laugh, and it made the tension in my shoulders release.

"She's right," he said. "Imagine just walking into all of this shit. It must be a serious mindfuck."

I nodded, relieved someone understood what was going on with me.

"It happened to each of us at one point or another," Shane interjected.

"Yeah, but not quite as abruptly as it did for Brynn." Dom looked at me. "At least we already knew each other, from growing up in the same town. We had the home-field advantage."

Shane shrugged as if *that* detail didn't matter. He'd clearly been impacted deeply by this group and their past projects, and I was super curious to know more about that. It was like he knew something important but wasn't ready to share it.

Poorva and Dom seemed more confident in their roles within the secret group. Maybe they'd known about their gifts longer, or perhaps their gifts were less intense than Shane's. I watched him as he struggled to look comfortable in the situation. His anxious response from being so close to the woods made me nervous.

"So, should we talk about what our approach will be?" Poorva asked. "Particularly, now that we've been divided into teams."

Shane's head popped up. "I know. I hate that it's a team thing. I'd much rather stick together." He lifted his eyes to mine for a second.

I agreed with him. I didn't want to become divided either.

"I know. Me too," I said. "Maybe there's a way we can do this together, but then present to Ms. Kelly in teams at the end. That way, she'll still be happy with the outcome."

Dom shook his head. "I don't know. I think she wants us to take two separate approaches. That's the whole point."

Poorva agreed. "True. It's part of her plan. Maybe she knows that separating us will be useful."

"Or necessary," I stated, wondering if it was a safety protocol.

"True." Poorva nodded.

Shane crossed his arms and shook his head. "In case something bad happens to one team," he huffed. "Then the other team is still in the game..."

His voice was cut off by Dom's.

"Yeah, to finish it," Dom blurted.

I swallowed hard, praying they were exaggerating about what could possibly happen. But they'd been through these projects before, so their worry came from a place of experience. That was what bothered me the most.

"Well, I think it's useful for us to meet up as a big group at times like this," I said, trying to hide the nervous shake in my voice. "Planning together is important."

Dom stood up. "Or not. And the best team wins."

Shane covered his eyes with one hand, shaking his head. "It's not the big game in the play-offs, Dom," he seethed. "It's not like there's a trophy or a scholarship attached to this one. I think we need to keep focus on the goal of the project."

Dom hovered his height over Shane. "And what is that, exactly?"

Shane stood, glaring into Dom's face, and then stepped out of his shadow. "We don't know yet. But safety in numbers makes the most sense."

"Chicken shit," Dom mumbled.

Shane shot back into Dom's personal space.

"Fuck you, Dom," Shane spat.

Their faces came so close I was sure they'd touch. The tension between the two energized the air around us, causing my heart to race.

I stared at Poorva in complete shock at the turn of events. Tempers had flared quickly, and they didn't seem to be backing down. It was clear there was history between the two, and it only took a small comment to set them off.

They squared off as if provoking the other to make a move.

"Cut the shit, you guys. You're already allowing the divide-and-conquer tactic to take hold?" I moved in between them. "We're one team. And we need to stay that way."

I glared at each of them, waiting for a back-down. Neither of them released the air that pumped out their chests until the next moment.

A louder turkey call flew out from the woods, causing us all to jump.

The new rush of adrenalin shifted our focus back the forest, and the guys moved away from their confrontational stances.

All eyes stared into the darkness of the old trees, considering whatever it might be that was lurking in their eerie shadows.

It already had a hold on us.

We all knew the creepy cackling had to be a turkey or some other form of wildlife, but that wasn't enough to keep our imaginations from running wild.

At least it was enough to distract Dom and Shane from their rivalrous confrontation. They'd stepped away from each other, allowing the conflict to deescalate.

"So, you guys know about the legend of the Dark Witch, right?" Poorva whispered.

Shane shot a narrowed glance at her that, if looks could kill, well, yeah, she'd be a goner.

Dom chuckled. "Yup. She eats kids, right? Just like in Hansel and Gretel."

I stared at all of them and swallowed hard. "The Dark Witch?" I muttered.

Hearing the words pass my lips made it sound scarier, almost like saying it would conjure her.

Witches freaked me out. Dark witches sounded even creepier.

And woods scared me, too.

This project sucked.

I squeezed my eyes shut, wishing it all away.

Poorva continued, "Something like that, Dom. Is that what they told you when you were a kid?"

"I don't remember." He kicked pebbles away from his feet. "I never paid attention."

"Yeah, right," Shane mumbled.

His antagonizing remark surprised me like he was poking the bee's nest, inviting more trouble with Dom. It was clear Shane wasn't intimidated by him in the least, and I was sure he was one of the few.

Before Dom had a chance to respond to his taunt, I interjected. "So, what's the legend?"

Poorva glanced into the woods and then at us. "Well, I've always been fascinated by the story, so I've tried to learn as much as possible. My mom has a friend who likes to talk about it, so any time she's over, I always listen. Once she's had enough wine, the stories get really good."

"So, you believe in that shit?" Dom spat.

Poorva cringed, feigning her wounds. "Kind of," she said. "Like, I'm here right now. Shitting my pants. Must mean I believe *something*."

I let out a nervous laugh.

Truth was, I was shitting my pants too, and was relieved to find out I wasn't the only one.

"Anyway," she continued, looking at me like I was the one who needed the information the most. "The woods are supposed to be haunted by a witch trapped in limbo. The woods are her territory to roam, and supposedly, she preys on young souls, using their energy to either cross over or come back. And she's pissed off, basically. Like, she was wronged in her lifetime and now has a twisted vengeance to boot."

My heart sank to my feet, causing light-headedness.

"That sucks," I murmured, staring into the forest, imagining what the Dark Witch might look like.

I squeezed my eyes shut to erase the horrifying images I'd created, most of which included bony fingers, stringy gray hair, a long, bent nose, and a wicked laugh that could stir the dead.

"Yeah, it does suck," Shane agreed, likely picturing similar images.

"Yup," Dom said. "It's a creepy bedtime story to keep kids out of the woods. And it works like a charm. For the most part." He turned his attention to me. "Sometimes, kids start to feel brave or want to show off in front of their friends, and they wander in. That's when the news reports of missing children start flying."

Poorva jumped in. "The boys who went missing last week were gone for only a few hours, but the town always flies into a panic, assuming the worst. All because of the one boy who never came out."

Shane and Dom dropped their eyes as if out of respect for the dead. Their somber responses made it seem like they might have known him.

I looked at Poorva with distinct apprehension, not really wanting to hear more, but having to.

"It was seven or eight years ago," she told me. "He went into the woods with a friend but never came out. He was never found. Lost without a trace."

My heart rate accelerated, making me shake. How could a town ever recover from a tragedy like that? It would leave a gaping wound that festered, never healing.

And that was exactly what it had done. I'd felt it from the moment I arrived to this town. Like a blanket of despair shrouding every part, it hit my soul deeply. No flower gardens or celebratory flags down Main Street could hide the truth from me. This town was cursed.

"That's awful," I said. "That poor family."

Shane fell back onto a bench with a lifeless thud.

Poorva looked at him briefly, then back at me. "I think Shane knew him," she whispered, though we could all hear.

I turned to Shane in horror and stepped over to him. No wonder he was so sensitive about being here. If he knew that boy in any way, it would be devastating to him.

He remained silent with his head down.

I glanced at Dom, and he just shrugged and looked away. My eyebrows pulled together tight from his cool apathy.

"That's a horrible story," I said. "I think this project is too much. It's too real. We shouldn't have to do something like this."

Then Shane rose to his feet and turned toward the entrance to the woods. "No. We *have* to do this," he stated with conviction. "We're the exact ones who need to."

"Okay, wait. Hold on a second," I reached for Shane's sleeve to stop him from storming straight into the woods. "I agree we need to explore this place further, especially since people have been hurt, but we need to be smart about it. Like, we need to be prepared, so nothing goes wrong."

"I have a bat in the back of my Jeep," Dom interjected.

Poorva spat out a laugh, spitting even more from the effort of stifling it.

Her faux pas hit me in my funny bone, and I cracked up, too. It was more from the stress of our nerves than anything else, but clearly Dom's ego had been hit by the giggles.

"What?" He exaggerated his innocent tone. "You were hoping for something sharper, like a stake?"

"No, asshole," Shane scoffed. "She's not talking about weapons. She's talking about our skills."

The air was still tense between them, and I wondered more about their unstable history. They must have had a laundry list a mile long, judging from the brittle air between them. It was like it could shatter at any moment like thin glass.

"Right," I interjected. "I'm not sure what you guys are even capable of, like, how strong your powers are. And, well, I'm not even sure what *I* can do." I glanced at each of them. "Is this something we can at least talk about? Or is it some big secret that everyone keeps hidden? I seriously have no clue. But I'll tell you guys whatever you want to know."

Dom's thick eyebrows rose up, creating deep lines in his forehead. "Really?" His tone teased me.

Poorva jabbed at his ribs and stepped closer to me. "We don't keep our skills a secret. You'll definitely see more in Ms. Kelly's X-block. We push ourselves to new limits with her guidance. That's where we learn the most about each other. And ourselves." She smirked to one side. "My skills started with aura reading. I can pick up on energy around people, sometimes in color. It seemed to come from the chakras."

"They talk about those in yoga classes," I said.

Poorva nodded. "Right. They're the vital force centers in each person. I've always been able to access that energy in people."

"Don't just leave her hanging on that," Shane interjected.

Poorva shot a side-eye at him and then looked back to me. "Ms. Kelly helped me strengthen my aura reading, and during that time, she helped me access more."

"More what?" I pressed.

"Just, more," she said, dropping her eyes to the ground.

Dom cracked his knuckles. "Yeah, Ms. Kelly helped us all access more, you could say. She's got a knack for training sensitives to access their full psychic ability."

My eyebrows shot up from the words 'psychic ability'. It just seemed so mystical. I could live with being called a sensitive, but I wasn't so sure about becoming a full-blown psychic.

"Even if you don't necessarily want to," Dom added.

His comment made me wonder if he wished he never even knew what he was capable of. Maybe it frightened him. It made sense, though, hiding behind his bravado and big-man-on-campus image. There was a good chance he was just as lost as the rest of us.

"What can you do?" I asked, holding nothing back.

Dom stepped back from the circle.

Shane let out a laugh like I'd just stepped out of line. "Damned if we knew," he blasted. "Keeps it to himself. Only Ms. Kelly knows."

Poorva smiled at Dom. "Yeah, but he knows how to determine when it's necessary to use it. He doesn't let us down. Ever."

I nodded and slowly turned to Shane. I didn't dare ask him what his skill was. I'd already screwed up by asking Dom, and now I decided it was time to exercise a little more secret-academy-etiquette.

Shane grinned and stood taller. "No secrets here," he said, puffing out his chest. "Clairsentience. Look it up." He wiggled his eyebrows.

I repeated the word in my mind a dozen times to be sure I'd remember it. My evening was sure to be filled with searches involving 'clear-sentence-something' and chakras.

Although, I was certain my research on Poorva's gift would be short-sighted. It was clear she had something else she wasn't ready to share. At first, I thought maybe she was uncomfortable with it, like Dom, but then I couldn't help wonder if it was because she was on the other team. Keeping her strongest gift a secret might strengthen their side.

I snuck a quick glimpse at her. She didn't seem to have any ulterior motive. The vibe she sent was authentic, so I decided just see what would happen from here.

My phone buzzed to life, and the four of us jumped and shot our attention into the woods. With nervous giggles, we turned to the true source of the interruption. Blake's name glowed on my screen.

"Blake's FaceTiming," I said, hitting the green circle.

His face appeared, and I answered while scanning all of our faces for him to see.

"Hey, Blake. We're all still here. What's up?" I said.

"Hey guys," he replied with a curt tone. "Um, don't panic or anything, but..."

His image froze, and the sound went dead. The four of us huddled closer and stared at the phone. A moment later, it came back to action.

Blake was still speaking as if not realizing he'd paused. "...So, basically, I think you should get the fuck out of there. Like, now!"

His alarmed tone shot urgency through us all, and before I could even respond, we were moving to the cars.

"Wait, Blake. We couldn't hear what you said before..." I panted into my phone while jumping into Poorva's car.

With my gaze over my shoulder, terrified something would be seething out of the woods to take us away, I caught Dom's eye.

"Text me," he called, and two seconds later, his tires shot gravel into the air as he barreled away.

Shane was in gear just as quickly and slowed as he pulled up along our car. "Go," he shouted, moving his RAV over to make room for us to pass.

Poorva fumbled with the keys and the gears and basically anything else that could waste valuable time.

"What the fuck?" Shane shouted through his open window. He glanced behind us toward the woods. "Go!"

Poorva knocked it into drive and gunned it. Our heart rates had hit near hysteria by the time we pulled out of the lot. Shane drove up right behind us practically hitting our bumper.

As I turned in my seat for one last look behind, I noticed a strange fog coming from the trees, almost like heavy gray smoke. It swirled from the wind off our cars, creating an opening into the trail, like an eerie invitation.

# CHAPTER 9

The group chat blew up for the rest of the night.

Blake tried to explain his cryptic FaceTime message to us by saying he had heard convoluted thoughts within our group that weren't ours. He said it seemed like someone else was there with us.

At first, I didn't know what to think of his quick texts—they left so much to interpretation. How would he know that someone else was present in our thoughts? It made no sense. But then Poorva sent me a private text with only one word.

Telepath.

So, Blake's skill was telepathy. It was no big surprise. He'd used it on me when we first met in advisory. Somehow he knew what I had been thinking in the group and was able to tell me what I needed to know, without saying a word.

Now that his ability was confirmed, all I could think about was him reading my private thoughts, like the ones I never wanted anyone to hear.

I typed back to Poorva.

*Nooooo that's so embarrassingggggg*

She replied.

*IKR u get used to it*

I jumped back into the group chat, trying to ignore this new layer of exposure. And, honestly, I didn't know if I'd ever be able to look Blake in the eye again. It was crazy to think that he knew all of our thoughts and insecurities. Our dreams and our fantasies. I just had to learn to block it out like the rest of the group did.

I focused back on my questions and the adrenaline rush we'd all experienced. By the time we'd exhausted replaying all the events from the woods, including my story of the fog and Blake's warning of a mystery visitor, it was midnight.

We reluctantly left the chat to go to sleep, and I couldn't help but wonder if Courtney had been reading all of it or if she truly didn't access social media at all. I was sure she would have been intrigued to have heard everything that had happened.

My mind raced for the next two hours while I stared at my ceiling. The thrill of our little adventure awakened a part of me that had been dormant for a very long time. My curiosity piqued to full height, and I couldn't settle my thoughts from running in every possible direction.

Blake's telepathy, the fog from the woods, discovering my own abilities, and Courtney's silence. Everything twisted through my head, creating a tangled web of confusion that left me with a migraine.

My eyes popped open to the morning sun, and I hadn't even realized I'd fallen asleep. Judging by my groggy brain, I knew I was firing on maybe three hours. I dragged myself through my morning routine and fell out the door.

Seeing everyone again was my priority, but keeping our group a secret was the obstacle.

I'd have to get through the next several days leading up to X-block, pretending like I hardly knew them.

It would be torture.

Each school day blurred into the next as I navigated the vicious social hierarchy of high school and the desire to spend time with my secret team. They told me in our text chat that we had to be careful to not appear too close with one another, bringing unwanted attention to our project. Our group had a reputation of being odd and suspicious, which brought negative curiosity and scrutiny to it.

They told me it had happened before when there was suspicion that the group had strange motives. Some thought the purpose of the group was to experiment on psychedelic drugs like DMT, others thought it was worshipping the devil, but whatever the accusations were, they only placed more scrutiny on Ms. Kelly.

And she was the best thing the school had.

Ms. Kelly knew how to connect with student in a real way. But it didn't go unnoticed by me how the principal looked at her with judgment and how the secretary followed suit. Their critical glares sent clear messages to me of disapproval. They didn't like her for some reason. She just didn't fit the cookie-cutter-educator-robot role, and it brought frowns upon her.

So, our job was to protect her.

It was the unwritten, unspoken code of the UMAs.

Ms. Kelly didn't realize this was our primary focus, but we all knew it had to be. Everyone's worst fear included either our group being disbanded, and each of us sent to a different X-block advisory, or Ms. Kelly being sandbagged by her haters and fired. We had to remember never to underestimate the power of the haters. Their agendas were clear and concise and involved stopping anyone who appeared to have more success than themselves. They were miserable trolls motivated by their own negativity and thrived on seeing the failure of others.

We were an easy target.

Whenever we were together, our group was close-knit, trusting, and powerful. It was apparent we held some form of power that made others notice us—making them jealous. That was what made us a target.

So, laying low in school made good sense, but it totally sucked.

And it didn't end there.

We had to be cautious not to be seen together out of school, as well. We'd always have the excuse that we were working on our community service project, but that would only be useful once or twice. Everyone knew all the X-block projects were a joke and didn't require that much out-of-school effort.

All but ours.

And so, as the days rolled past, I counted the hours to the next X-block.

∽

Finally.

One more day until advisory.

The wait between our secret society meetings was brutal. They were all I could think about, and this next one, in particular, was critical. I had so many questions and was dying to figure out how to tap further into my own abilities. But mostly, I needed to know more about our project and how we were going to survive it.

Heading to my first-period class, I passed the main office and nearly bumped into Ms. Kelly. I'd rarely seen her outside of the guidance office and was surprised.

"Oh, hi," I said.

"Good morning, Brynn." Ms. Kelly smiled. "How are your classes going?"

Okay, we were going to play it cool. Right.

"They're great, thanks," I replied. "Tons of homework, but that's to be expected, I suppose."

"I bet." She stepped closer and dropped her volume. "Stay alert today. Something doesn't feel right."

Then she moved to another group of students, greeting them with her welcoming smile.

I remained frozen in my spot for a second, and then without looking at her again, I continued to my class.

It was a warning of some kind, and I had no clue what to do with it.

As I entered my English class, I shot straight to Dom. He caught the unsettled look in my eye and moved to the window with me.

"What's up?" he said, glancing over his shoulder.

I followed his gaze to be sure no one was paying attention to us.

Everyone was paying attention to us.

"Shit. I'll tell you later," I whispered. "But I was told to be careful today. Something's up."

"What the fuck does that mean?" he pressed.

"I have no idea." I glanced at the students in the room, all watching us. "I'll text you."

And I bombed for my desk.

Before I could drop by backpack by my chair, Laney stepped in my way. Her crony, Liv, hovered by her side with her permanent bitch-face in full operation.

"Nice purple hair," Liv mocked, looking me up and down.

"Nice inferential analysis on Great Expectations," I retorted, feeling a twang of guilt for calling her out on her complete buffoonery in class yesterday. But she asked for it.

I heard a chuckle rumble behind me from Dom.

Liv blinked as if catching a bullet—a bullet that made no sense to her.

Laney tipped her head. "Don't tread where you don't belong, Douglas," she said, narrowing her eyes on me.

I shook my head, dismissing her comment, and sat down. Ignoring these girls was my only defense at the moment.

As Mr. Benson entered the room, Laney and Liv went back to their seats, but not without sending dagger glares my way the entire time.

I held my phone under my desk and typed to Dom.

*What the hell is Laney's problem*

Heat radiated from my face as I stewed in anger. Now that she was gone, I thought of a thousand better comebacks, as always. What the hell did she mean anyway? *Don't tread where you don't belong.* Was that her way of telling me to get away from Dom?

I watched Dom's shoulders round in as he typed under his desk.

*She's threatened by u*

He typed again.

*Its actually fun to watch*

My face reddened again with fumes as I typed.

*Um no. Not funny. Kind of a pain in the ass*

Mr. Benson called attendance as I watched Dom typing back.

*Shes intimidated*

Send.

*Ur comfortable in ur own skin and she hates that*

Send.

*She knows theres something different about u*

send

*Oh and ur pretty*

Send.

*That makes u a triple threat*

Send.

I stared at his string of texts and froze.

"Brynn. Brynn Douglas," Mr. Benson's voice punched me in the face.

"Oh, here," I stated, more loudly than I'd intended.

My face burned as I felt Dom's eyes on me. I lifted my gaze and met his. He waited for a reaction, and I smiled quickly, then dropped my eyes to my desk.

My thumbs hovered over my phone, stumbling on what to type back.

Finally, they moved over the letters.

*Well I wish she'd back off*

Send.

*And thanks*

Send.

∽

I stumbled through the rest of my day on cloud nine.

It was stupid.

How one boy saying I was pretty could have such an effect on me was ridiculous. I hated myself for reacting like the-giddy-chick-who-the-hot-guy-just-paid-attention-to, especially when much more important things were going on.

A guilty smile crossed my face.

Even though I knew I was being an idiot, I couldn't help it.

I kept an eye out for Dom after the last bell, but when I didn't see him, I assumed he had football practice or something else to do. It was probably just as well. I didn't need any more opportunities to make a fool of myself, and with this level of blushing distraction, I was in a high danger zone for dumbass behaviors.

I needed Poorva's steady hand to keep me stabilized, but she was gone too. With study hall last block, she flexed her National Honor Society privilege and signed out early.

I resigned myself to the fact that I'd be walking home alone and was strangely fine with that. As much as I liked a ride when it presented itself, it felt right to walk today. Funny thing was, though, instead of barreling out of the school to escape the prison, I lingered longer than necessary in the bathroom.

Waiting for the student lot to empty out was a priority. The last thing I needed was to have Laney and her friends bomb past me in her mom's Beemer, kicking up dust all over my face. Just no.

After ten minutes of scrolling through Instagram, I stood from my seat on the commode in the girl's room and shook life back into my tingling legs. Poking my head out, I glanced through the empty halls and then made my way for the front doors.

Glancing through the main office windows as I passed by, I caught a glimpse of Ms. Kelly flipping through some files. She noticed me passing and nodded with a hopeful smile and a knowing look in her eye. It was as if she knew my plans for the afternoon before I even did.

I brushed off the strange feeling and pushed through the double doors. Squinting from the assault of bright sunlight, I thumped down the steps while hoisting my pack on my shoulder. The metal gates at the entrance to the school remained open, and I stepped through them, setting out toward home.

Without warning, a familiar sickening twist of anxiety entered my gut as I wondered if Mom would be home. It was sad that I had to worry about such a thing, but that was only natural for me. She'd been particularly grumpy these past few days, and I hoped maybe something had shifted to improve her mood. I'd gone through the unstable emotional rollercoaster of her being nice, rude, aggressive, passed out, or whatever. It sucked. I'd much prefer a more 'normal mom' that wanted to hear about my day, have a healthy snack ready, or was busy working at a successful job. Any of those would be better, in my opinion.

But then I figured, maybe I wouldn't be who I was today if it weren't for her twisted ways. I had to practically raise myself, and that must have created a thicker skin for me. Maybe I'd cope better in life as a result. My hippie guidance counselor from my past school called it grit. At first, it sounded like an insult or something I didn't want, but now I understood the reference better. Maybe perseverance wasn't such a bad thing. And perhaps it would come in handy now.

Walking along the main road, I glanced at a row of shops and businesses as I got closer to my house. I hadn't had much time to explore the places around me and wondered if maybe there was a cool second-hand store where I could go thrifting. Then my attention was pulled to a large white church that I hadn't noticed before. It was a typical historic building to see in a town like this, and so I'd never paid it much attention.

Until now.

Because I could swear, I was staring at Shane's car parked in the lot along the side of the church. All by itself.

The blue RAV had the same faded Lakefield High decal on the back window.

I knew it had to be his.

My mind jumped to every possible explanation of what Shane would be doing in a church, and I let out an audible huff with each option. None of them making sense.

It was the middle of the day when no services were scheduled, judging by the empty lot, and he'd never mentioned a strong affinity for the church. Quite the opposite, actually. He'd mentioned at one point that he didn't practice his religion at all.

Before I had another moment to process more ideas of why he might be there, I was crossing the street, heading straight for the sprawling marble steps of the church.

I was determined to know if he was inside. And if he was, I wanted to know what the hell he was doing in there.

As I reached the top of the steps, my eyes moved up the height of the arched black doors, and I pulled on the handle of one of them. The door opened, sending an echo into the vast space within. Stepping into the foyer, I cringed from the booming sound the door made as it closed behind me.

Then, only silence.

A sense of guilt washed over me—the one you get when you know you should go to church but don't. And then the feeling of entering a sacred space when feeling less than holy, it was unsettling to say the least. I tried to shake it off but knew in my heart I shouldn't be in there, not without cleansing my soul first anyway.

I stepped into the enormous space and gazed up at the ornate vaulted ceilings in awe of the grandiose construction, and then I studied the humble simplicity of the front altar. A huge exhale fell out of me as I realized it was a safe space. It felt okay for me to enter.

Then my eyes shifted along the numerous rows of wooden pews to the front corner of the church. Two people sat, huddled in the shadows, whispering in deep concentration.

I froze, not wanting to disturb them in whatever they were discussing. Their intensity vibrated off of them and struck me in the heart. Whatever they were talking about, it was emotional and heavy. The burden weighed on me instantly, and I struggled to get a full breath.

I took a step closer in curiosity, and my foot thumped the wooden edge of a pew, sending a tremor through the expansive space.

The two people shot their attention to me in surprise, and I stood without a flinch, staring into Shane's eyes.

# CHAPTER 10

A twang of shame shot through me as Shane stood and walked up the aisle toward me. I hadn't meant to interrupt him—especially in such a sacred space.

And now I wasn't even sure why I had walked into the church in the first place. It was none of my business what Shane did with his free time, but it just took me by surprise that he'd be the religious type. I couldn't help but think he had gone in there for something else.

"Hey, what are you doing here?" he asked, taking my elbow and leading me back into the foyer.

I turned to look at the man still seated in the first pew in front by the altar. He watched us with a peaceful smile.

"Sorry," I whispered. "I didn't mean to interrupt you. I saw your car, and I was curious to see what you were doing." I shook my head and put my hand over my eyes.

"Really?" His eyebrows lifted.

Oh, great. Now I looked like I was stalking him. Shit.

"Well, I don't know. It just didn't seem like the type of place you would typically go." I fumbled on my words. "And I was in no hurry to get home."

He huffed. "What? I don't look like a faithful believer to you?"

I shrugged one shoulder. "Not *this* type of believer." I glanced around at the religious icons.

"Touché," he said with a nod. "You got that right. I have a friend here. I like to stop by for a chat once in a while."

"A church friend?" I teased.

He narrowed his eyes at me. "The minister, actually. He's a good guy. Old family friend."

He took a step closer to the door.

"Oh, jeez." I grimaced briefly from my poor choice of words. "Sorry I interrupted you two."

"No worries. We were done anyway. I never stay for very long. It gets... challenging." He pushed one of the big black doors open. "Come on. Let's get out of here."

We moved down the massive marble steps and onto the pavement. I glanced in the direction of my house, not wanting to have to go there.

Shane watched me, then turned his attention to his car, jingling his keys. "Wanna go for a coffee? There's an awesome cafe in the square."

The temptation was huge. I hesitated for a second, not wanting to send him any mixed signals, and then realized, it was fine. Of course we could go for coffee. And we had so much to talk about, it made perfect sense. And plus, he knew I was a senior, so that would be enough to deter any awkwardness.

"Yeah, sure," I said, pushing off my annoying inner dialogue.

He stood taller and grinned.

"Cool." He clicked his keys, and the car beeped. "Get in."

I threw my backpack in the back seat and climbed in shotgun. His car smelled like a mix of oak, peppermint, and well, him. The scent opened up my senses and somehow allowed me to know him better.

He was kind and honest.

He loved his family.

And, he was deeply frightened of something.

The information flooded me, and I held my breath. How could a smell trigger so much information—all of which I knew to be true?

He turned to me and caught my wide-eyed stare.

"What?" he asked. "Did I do something?"

"No, I just... I just got a strange sensation." I continued to gaze at him. "It's weird. Like I can sense things about you."

"Shit. Are you serious?" He twisted to face me directly. "It's your skill. Like, it's opening up."

"Maybe." I squinted my eyes, trying to perceive more.

"Sometimes, in close spaces, it's easier to read a person," he said. "I mean, like now, it's almost like cheating, because I'm pretty good at this, but I know exactly how you are feeling. You don't want to go home. And not just because you need a coffee fix." His face grew somber. "It makes you feel empty inside. Like you're a visitor in your own house. You think you're not wanted there."

A lump swelled in my throat. I wanted to punch him for knowing so much. He put into words everything I'd felt for a lifetime.

"How do you know that?" I choked.

"I'm sorry. I'll stop," he said, twisting front again. He started the car. "I didn't mean to pry." He glanced at me again. "It's just very easy for me to read you right now. I'm not sure why."

"Clairsentience?" I asked.

He took a double-take. "Exactly." And then he pulled out of the lot.

"But the way you put it into words," I mumbled. "Like, *feeling like a visitor in my own home.* I didn't even realize that." I watched his focus remain on the road, knowing it was really still on me. "Okay. What else?"

I couldn't let him stop there. He might as well keep throwing the punches. Get it over with.

He glimpsed at me for a second, then back at the road.

He swallowed and said, "You feel alone." He hesitated. "And you think if you act like you don't care, it won't hurt as much."

My air rushed out of me like I'd been punched right in the gut.

"Okay, stop," I whimpered. "Shit."

"Sorry. That last part was too easy," he laughed. "The purple hair's a dead giveaway."

Oh, now he comments about my hair.

I dropped my jaw and gawked at him. "Are you making fun of

my hair?"

He chuckled. "Um, yeah." He shot a quick glance at me from the corner of his eye, probably checking if I was about to hit him. "I mean, come on, everyone knows that trick."

My jaw fell open.

"You asshole!" I swatted at him. "I like my hair."

"No, I do, too," he apologized. "I'm just saying..."

"Shut up. Just change the subject," I jabbed. "There's no recovering from that one."

I couldn't help my smile from spreading across my face. No one had ever called me out on my hair before—at least, not so blatantly.

And he wasn't wrong. So, I had to give him some credit for his honesty.

"Sorry. I don't know when to keep my mouth shut sometimes," he murmured. "When the information floods like that, I just can't control it."

"No, that's actually amazing. You know, your ability," I said. "I'm feeling rather exposed right now, but super impressed at the same time."

I blinked, attempting to shade any other thoughts or feelings I might be having. If he exposed me any further, I would just have to change schools again.

"It's also torture," he added.

My smile fell away, and I glanced at him, waiting for more.

He continued. "I feel other people's sorrow. Deeply." He glanced back at the church. "As if it were my own."

Shane pulled into a spot along the town common by the gazebo, and we hopped out of the RAV. I'd been tongue-tied for the second half of the ride after hearing about his burden—feeling other people's grief. It was a horrible sentence to have to live with, and as I stared at the sharp angles of his jaw and cheekbones, I noticed the lines of worry and sorrow around his eyes. He carried it with him, always.

He stepped off the sidewalk and cut across the green lawn of the town square.

"Come on. This way," he called to me.

I followed him, and we walked past a tall monument decorated with small American flags stuck in the ground around its base. He hopped up the steps of the gazebo in the center of the common and moved to the far side of it.

Curious about what he was doing, I climbed the steps and joined him.

"It's a pretty town," I said, gazing at the shops around the perimeter of the square.

"Yeah, they try to make it look like an All-American town," he agreed. "Like in the movies. But, like anything else, beneath the facade is the truth. And it's not pretty."

I turned to him and studied his face, wondering what he knew. Probably a lot.

He glanced at me and shrugged. "Maybe every town has its secrets," he added.

"I don't know," I said. "I've lived in a lot of towns, and even though this one if by far the nicest, its also by far the strangest."

He laughed. "Yup. Figures."

He nudged me to follow him. We hopped off the gazebo and headed toward a corner shop with a sign hanging off the side that said *Cafe on the Common.*

"I hope you're not the 'hazelnut' or 'vanilla bean' type of coffee drinker," he joked. "That would be really disappointing."

"Oh, please. Are you serious?" I rolled my eyes. "I like my coffee to taste like coffee."

He reached for the door, ready to pull it open, and gazed through the stenciled glass. He dropped his grip on the door and hesitated.

"What is it?" I watched his face turn ashen.

I peered through the window and surveyed the inside of the shop. Instantly, my eyes fell on her, and I pulled away from the door.

Laney was in there.

I had no idea what was bothering Shane, but whatever it was, I had no problem going somewhere else. Laney was enough to make me lose my interest in one of my biggest addictions.

"Let's go somewhere else," Shane said.

"Fine by me," I agreed.

We crossed back over to the common and climbed back into the gazebo. We sat this time, enjoying the shelter of the sidewalls of the arbor.

I wondered what had deterred him so drastically from entering the cafe. Sure, my arch-nemesis was in there, but was it possible his was too? Then I realized the scope of her evil and figured she must have gotten her claws into him also.

"Was it Laney?" I asked.

His eyes darted to mine and then down onto the wooden floor beneath us. He stared at the names and figures carved into the planks.

"Yeah," he finally said. "She's kind of a real bitch."

I huffed. "No shit."

He lifted his gaze. "Wait, you already know her, too?"

"Yup. She's in my Lit class, and unfortunately, she goes out of her way to torture me." I exhaled. "I didn't want to go into the cafe either, once I saw her in there."

He shook his head. "That sucks. I wish she didn't have that kind of power over other people."

I nodded. But at the same time, I tried to figure out what power she had over him. I mean, he was a year below her, and no threat, obviously, to her queen bee status, so it made no sense that he was a target of hers as well.

"She's probably threatened by you," he said.

I pressed my lips to the side and narrowed my eyes. I'd heard that one before.

"No, seriously," he added, then shrugged. "I guess it doesn't matter, though."

He was right. It didn't matter why. It only mattered that she treated people like shit and needed to stop.

"And what does she have against *you*?" I asked.

He swallowed as if contemplating how much to say.

"She has a way of always being there when something goes wrong like it was part of her master plan all along," he murmured.

I bent my head, waiting for more. Shane looked into my eyes, and the warmth of his gaze told me he was ready to trust me.

He went on. "It was a long time ago, but the day I went into those woods, on a dare, she was there. She wasn't the one who actually dared me, but it was as if she'd orchestrated the whole thing. And ever since, I've felt her presence, lingering, like she had a hold on me, permanently." He shuddered to shake off the uncomfortable feeling. "She knows it too. I can tell by the smirk on her face any time she sees me."

Something powerful happened to Shane in the woods that day. Whatever it was, he needed to tell us. If we were going to explore the legend of the Dark Witch, or whatever it was that was going on in there, he would need to tell us what he knew. Especially if Laney had any inkling of it as well.

"That sucks," I said. "Whatever it was that happened to you in those woods, it sucks that she had any part of it. It only gives her more power."

"Exactly," he said. "Once she knows a person's weakness, they're fucked."

My phone buzzed, and I checked it. Dom's name lit up.

*Ur with Shane?*

My eyes widened.

"How the hell does Dom know we're together?" I blasted, without time to filter my comment.

"Of course," Shane seethed. "What a prick." He glanced at my phone. "She must have seen us and texted him."

"What? Why?" I shook my head at the absurdity.

"Hell if I know," he barked. "She thinks she owns him and uses him like a puppy dog. It's painful to watch."

I shook my head. "I just don't know why she cares so much." I looked over the sideboard back toward the cafe.

"She cares...," Shane started. "Because she knows more than she should." He glanced around us, then whispered, "She's dangerous."

There was only one thing to do, and that was to get out of the town square, asap. Hanging out anywhere in the vicinity of Laney was a definite no.

"Let's go somewhere else then," I nudged him. "Away from here."

His eyebrows lifted at my suggestion. "Where?"

"I don't know. Back to the entrance to the woods?" I suggested. "Not to go in, or anything. But just to see it again, in full daylight this time. I want to see if that weird fog is still there."

Shane bit the skin around his pinky nail. "Yeah, okay, I guess."

His apprehension was obvious, and I assumed it must be from his bad experience there. Or maybe he thought we should only go there with the others. Either way, I wanted to hear more about what happened to him in the woods that day, and this was the best way I could think of.

We headed back to the car and made no attempt to hide the fact that we checked over our shoulders more than once to be sure Laney was nowhere to be seen. It was annoying how she had so much control over us, but at this point, we weren't willing to fight the invisible battle. Instead, we hopped into his car and did our best to forget about her as we blasted his playlist as loud as it would go.

Within minutes, we were pulling up to the parking area at the edge of the woods. I turned off my tracker on Snap by instinct. It just seemed like the right thing to do. I barely used the app, but that didn't stop me from knowing it was the best stalking tool around.

"Shut off Snap maps," I told Shane. "We don't need any of the others stalking us and finding out we came here again without them."

"Good call," he said, fiddling with his phone.

We climbed out and walked over to the benches.

Before we even sat down, he murmured, "I used to have a crush on her."

His discomfort with the statement oozed from his shrunken posture.

I shot my attention to him. "Who?"

"Laney."

My gut twisted. I wasn't sure why, but it annoyed me to the core that her power was able to go that far.

"Shit."

"I know," he huffed. "I was young. And dumb." He gazed into the opening of the trail to the woods. "She knew it, too, so just to fuck with me, she flirted for a few days and then asked me to take a walk with her. Here."

I stared at him, wishing the story would end before it reached the worst part.

"I was scared shitless of this place, of course, but at the time, all I could think was that Laney Rosco wanted to hang out with me." He shrugged. "Like I said, dumb kid."

My eyes fell. No matter how young someone was, a broken crush could be brutal.

"When was this?" I asked, wondering how old he had been.

"Seventh grade," he mumbled.

He must have been about twelve. The prime age to be totally trusting, following your heart, and then to have someone step on it without mercy.

"So, what happened?"

His back straightened as tension tightened his muscles, and his jaw clenched, creating a sharper angle to his profile.

"When I got here, she was hanging out, laughing with Dom and his friends. They all knew it was a setup and laughed at me for thinking I even had a chance with Laney." He dropped his eyes. "Yeah, that was kind of a low point for me."

I felt the sting of humiliation for him. My lips pressed together in anger. Laney was a total bitch.

"That sucks. I hate her even more now. If that's even possible." I grated my teeth.

Why the hell would she do that to him? Just to look cool in front of the jocks? It made no sense to me. It was clear she had them all wrapped around her finger from a young age, so why pick on Shane?

He took a breath, then went on.

"Before I could make my quick exit and get out of there, Dom dared me to go into the woods. They all knew I'd never want to go in there, especially alone. But with all of them jeering, I had no choice."

I closed my eyes, feeling his inner turmoil from that moment when he was in seventh grade. The fear. The humiliation. The courage to face his fear under pressure. And then his disappointment in himself for falling victim to their bullying. It tore at my soul to feel what he had gone through.

"So I went in," he continued, staring into the darkness of the trail. "I shouldn't have. I should have known better. But they left me no choice." His eyes fell, and he stared at the dirt. "I saw something in there that haunts me to this day. I can't erase it. I can't forget it. But as soon as I saw it, my senses exploded. Something erupted in me, either from fear or from anger, I can't be sure. But that was the day my supernatural abilities came into full power. Like a burst of energy."

My eyes widened, and I stared into the woods. Something in there triggered his psychic power. But what?

"So, there really *is* something in those woods." I shot my eyes all around the trees.

He nodded slowly and exhaled his pent up stress.

"Yes. There's something about the woods. Something scary," he said. "Something evil."

My jaw fell open as I searched for my next words. I had no idea what I could say to him that would make any sense. His story was wild and left me with so many questions. I wanted to know what he saw in there. What could have the ability to cause such fear? Or the power to unlock someone's psychic potential? At this point, all I wanted to do was comfort him and offer my support. I figured the rest would follow.

Just as I prepared to say the next thing that popped into my mind, I jumped from the sound of crushing gravel. Our heads whipped in the direction of the noise, and we stared as a black Jeep tore into the lot.

"Shit," Shane fumed. "What the fuck is he doing here?"

# CHAPTER 11

My eyes flew wide and glued themselves on Dom's form as he stormed over to us. His letterman jacket made him look massive, and I secretly rolled my eyes at its elitist symbolism.

"Pulling out all the stops, I see," Shane spat. "Dick jacket and all. What? Did we miss a game?"

"We all wore them today, asshole," he retorted.

Shane huffed. "That's even worse," he murmured, shaking his head.

I was slow on the draw to stop their squabbling, still in shock that he was even here.

"How did you find us?" I finally asked.

Dom pulled his glare off Shane and turned his eyes to me. His steely stare softened as his shoulders settled. He lifted his phone and shook it at me.

"But I turned off maps," I faltered.

"Not soon enough," he said. "Your bitmoji was last seen on the way here, traveling in a little red car."

Shane smacked his hand to his eyes and grimaced.

"Oh. Yeah," I mumbled. "We just didn't want to upset anyone, you know."

Dom nodded. "Yup. Well, you failed. I might not have noticed if you had replied to my text."

I glanced at him through narrowed eyes. Was he upset? I couldn't tell if he was exaggerating the situation or if he was actually brooding. I wasn't usually this clueless, but if I wasn't mistaken, he was acting like his ego had been bruised.

I shook my head to stop myself from over-thinking too much. First of all, I had no idea what these guys were capable of and if they could read my every thought. And second, where did I get off thinking the hottest guy in school had even an inkling of interest in me. Duh.

My gaze shot to Shane, and much to my horror, his confident stance had shifted to something else, now that Dom was here. He couldn't fully be himself around him, and I recognized the symptoms. I felt the same way around Laney and her friends—exposed, vulnerable, conquered. It sucked.

Before I could say anything to reassure Shane that I still wanted to hear the rest of his story, Dom butted in.

"So, something tells me you've been filling her head with your tales," he said to Shane. "Don't go making me out to be a monster, asshole. That was a long time ago." Then he turned to me. "Don't forget, there are two sides to every story."

Shit. Dom knew Shane was telling me the story. Who knew if it was his psychic abilities or if it was just plain obvious that Shane would tell it as a means to gain my favor, or at least to pull it away from Dom.

Feeling stuck in the middle was an understatement, and I was determined to extract myself from the vice grip.

"It doesn't matter now, you guys," I blurted. "Whatever happened is in the past. We just need to move forward and figure out what happened in these woods."

Dom shifted his weight with an uncertain gaze in his eyes. He wasn't ready to move on.

"Did he tell you the part where he fucked me over when he came barreling out of the woods? It was like he'd seen a ghost." Dom said. "Did he mention that?"

I turned to Shane. He hadn't had time to tell that part of the story yet. The part after his powers exploded. I had been giving him space, but then Dom showed up.

Shane's eyes locked on mine as if hoping to freeze time—stopping Dom from saying another word.

But it didn't work.

Dom went on, showing no mercy.

"When he burst out of the woods, like a frantic child, he crashed into me, sending lightning bolts of energy through my bones and every nerve." He shook his head as if feeling the impact again. "It fried my brain and all my insides, transforming me into something new. Something I couldn't control." He glared at Shane like he wanted to kill him. "And now, I have to live with it. As one of the freaks."

*What did he just call us?*

Okay, he just exposed his true colors.

He thought we were freaks.

But the joke was on him because he was one of us. He was a freak, too.

I turned my back to him and moved closer to Shane. He left me no choice but to show where my loyalty was.

"Jesus, Brynn," Dom backpedaled. "I didn't mean it like that."

Shane made his new confidence evident as he stood tall next to me.

"Is there another way to take it?" Shane shot back.

Dom dropped his head back and looked up to the sky. "I'm sorry. I just... I'm still trying to come to terms with this. I might seem like I have my shit together, but seriously, I feel like I could lose control at any moment. Like I might explode." His voice cracked. "Please..."

I couldn't help but feel bad for him. And it always drove me to a crazy place when a guy pleaded. It broke down my defenses instantly. Plus, it made sense that he would be unhappy with his unexpected situation. I decided to give him another chance.

I hoped Ms. Kelly knew how to help him. From the few times I'd seen them together, it had seemed like she understood what he was going through. There was an unspoken trust between the two, which left me hopeful that he would have the support he needed.

Feeling awkward, caught in the middle of the two of them, I dropped my eyes to look at my phone. Poorva's name lit up, and I tapped on it immediately.

*R u with dom*

Oh my god. Was that the only thing people texted these days—asking who I was with? And now all I could wonder was how *she* knew.

*Ya shane too*

I shook my head, waiting for her reply.

*A three way?*

I chuckled, relieved she didn't seem mad.

*Yup*

Then I added more.

*It wasn't planned just kinda happened going home now. text later?*

I'd fill her in on everything once I got home.

*Ya I think u should wait for ms kelly before going there again. She knows a lot about it. xblock.*

Either Dom had his Snap map on or Poorva had stronger powers of perception than I realized. Either way, she was right. I should wait for Ms. Kelly's guidance before coming back here again. There was too much unknown, and that made it very unpredictable. And it was obvious the power of this place was profound.

X-block couldn't come fast enough.

While dropping me off, Shane had offered to drive me to school the next morning. For some reason, I felt it better not to accept. I just didn't want to send any mixed messages and thought it best to remain in neutral territory.

I was glad I had Poorva as back up. She hadn't planned on picking me up, knowing that I liked the headspace during the walks to school, but she made an exception for this situation.

"Okay, spill," she commanded as I hopped in her car. "You are way too vague through texting."

I rolled my eyes with a loud sigh. "It's because there's nothing to tell. I bumped into Shane on the way home, so we went for coffee. The cafe was crowded, so instead, we drove to the woods to check it out again."

"Mhmm." Her tone reeked of disbelief.

"Dom tracked us on Snap before we were able to turn it off..."

"So you didn't want anyone to find you?" she shot with suspicion.

"Not like that, Poorva." I elbowed her. "We just didn't want the rest of UMA to know we went there again. It would only cause drama within the teams."

"What the hell is Ooma?" she spat.

I hesitated at my own comfort with the use of the term. I guess it just kind of stuck.

"You know, UMA, the name of the group chat," I said.

"Oh, right." She nodded with a knowing grin.

"What does it even mean?" I asked.

She chuckled. "Shane gave our advisory group a name a while back. He calls us the Urban Mystic Academy."

I nodded. "I get it. UMA."

I glanced out the window as we pulled into the student lot. My knee bounced in nervous anticipation. "I can't wait for X-block to hear more about our project."

She glanced at me from the corner of her eye with a judging smirk.

"I have a feeling you might be a little clueless about these projects she creates for us." Poorva parked and looked at me straight on. "They're our training. Like, no joke. So be prepared. It's usually pretty intense."

I listened to her words, feeling slightly reprimanded like I wasn't taking it serious enough. And her read on me wasn't far off. I had no idea what we were heading into, so, of course, I probably seemed like an over-enthusiastic newbie.

"Okay, yeah," I agreed. "I don't mean to be disrespectful or anything. I know there's something pretty powerful going on. But seriously, I'm just ready to start."

"I know." She nodded. "We were all like that on our first project. Eager to begin, excited to get started, but then there's terror. Running. Screaming. That sort of shit."

Oh, fuck. I had to keep reminding myself that we were different. Our mission wasn't typical of the average high-schooler. More was expected of us since we were gifted. And the other UMAs were light years ahead of me with their abilities and their experiences of the supernatural. They knew the rules of the secret group, and I had to yield to their knowledge—and Ms. Kelly's instruction. I had to follow her rules to the finest detail or anything and everything could go wrong.

Also, it was becoming clear that the UMAs were filtering the full details of what they'd accomplished in the past. Every time the stories began, they never quite finished. The others had probably been told not to share too much with me, that it was Ms. Kelly's role as the teacher to decide when and how much to tell.

I just had to be more patient, but it was so hard.

As we climbed out of the car, a voice called over to us.

"Who's excited to get started?" Dom teased as he came up behind me. "Just like each of us when we started on our first project." He rubbed the top of my head like I was a child.

I stared at him in shock as if he had overheard our entire conversation in the car. But that would have been impossible. The doors had been closed.

His teasing annoyed me to the core. Particularly because his words were true. I was the new, naive member of the group, and the fact that he found that entertaining was infuriating.

"Right," Poorva hissed. "You should probably know, Dom's hearing is insane. Never say anything within a mile of him if you don't want him to hear it."

I shot my eyes to his in disbelief.

"Kind of a curse, really," he said, looking around with a scowl.

"Most conversations are white noise to me. No one has anything of interest to say."

I froze for a second, reeling through my conversations in school, making sure I never spoke of Dom. Redness burned my cheeks as I panicked, getting lost in my various memories. I just prayed he hadn't heard all the things I was actually thinking. Some of it went far beyond PG-13, and I'd seriously have to move again if there was any chance he knew about any of it. But as for conversations, I figured I was probably safe if he heard any of those.

Able to breathe again, I looked him in the eyes and said, "I imagine that skill can come in handy at times."

He smirked with a nod. "Uh-huh."

I pulled my eyes away in an instant, unsure of what his tone might have meant. I sucked at these head games and bailed every time they began.

A moment later, Blake strolled along the sidewalk toward the front entrance and noticed us just before climbing the stairs. He bounded over, struggling with the weight of his backpack.

"Hey, twerp," Dom greeted him.

"Hey," he said, out of breath. "You guys need to stop messing around. Ms. Kelly's gonna get pissed."

"Messing around? Us?" Dom teased.

"You know what I mean. Just cut the crap," he shot. "And spread out. You're drawing too much attention to us. Wait 'til X-block." He darted away like he hardly knew us.

Poorva's eyes followed his stealthy retreat and then turned back to us. "He's probably right. We're supposed to be more discreet than this."

"Oh, you're brushing me away." Dom's hands flew up in defense.

"Actually, yes," Poorva said.

"Actually, no," Dom retorted. "Brynn and I have first period together. Makes more sense for you to be the one to disperse."

My eyes darted to hers in a desperate plea for her to stay.

"You suck," she said to him. "Whatever. Cause a shit-show of gossip. You're the one who'll have to live with it."

"Happily," he said, nudging me away from her, with an arrogant grin.

Poorva shook her head as if she were irritated, but then shot me a secret glance of 'oh my god!'. I swore I could hear her giddy voice bouncing through my brain. And I wanted to kill her for it as it shot nervous jitters through me.

Leaving the student lot behind us, Dom rattled on about last night's tedious homework as we aimed for the front steps of the school, but then my gaze fell on a student standing at the bottom of the stairs, staring at us.

Shane.

Oh no. I knew exactly how this must have looked—as if Dom had driven me to school, after Shane had offered. I smiled at him in panic, but he just turned and walked away.

"What's wrong with him?" Dom asked.

"No clue," I replied, keeping my focus on the stairs to be sure I didn't fall on my face.

Hurting Shane's feelings was the last thing I'd ever want to do. He didn't deserve it. Especially when what he thought he saw wasn't accurate, at all.

I dropped my head back, replaying what he must have witnessed, and I grimaced. There was probably no other interpretation in his mind.

I knew I could explain exactly what happened, but I wasn't sure if Shane would even listen at this point. And making him wait over two hours until X-block was just cruel. I decided to text him from English class in hopes he'd see it before our advisory meeting. I wanted our X-block to be as drama-free as possible.

But, at this point, it was pretty clear it was an impossible expectation.

∼

The minutes ticked on like eternity, but then the bell for X-block finally rang. Shane hadn't responded to my text, so I had no clue where things stood with him, but I could certainly guess.

Entering the guidance suite, Poorva and I went straight for the conference room. It was obvious we'd need privacy for today's X-block. I'd only wished we had hours for this session, instead of minutes.

Dom and Blake entered next like a most mismatched pair, followed by Courtney, who kept her head down.

Shane came in last and without a word, sat at the far side of the large table. He refused to lift his eyes to mine, and I fumed. I kept my gaze on him, hoping he'd feel the burn of my glare, but it seemed to have no affect, annoying me further.

"Um, have you checked your text messages?" I snarled across the table at him through clenched teeth.

Dom and Poorva turned their heads to me at the same time, but I kept my eyes on Shane.

His eyes lifted for a split-second, then Ms. Kelly entered.

"Good morning, everyone," she said with a firm tone. "I notice a fair bit of tension in the air. Eager to get started?" She glanced around the table.

"You could say that," Blake replied with sarcasm.

Ms. Kelly nodded as she surveyed the rest of us. It was clear that either Blake ratted us out or Ms. Kelly had a powerful sixth sense. Both options were valid, and either way, she knew what was up.

"You're getting ahead of yourselves," she said. "I like your enthusiasm. However, a few of you have ignored our code." She paused, waiting for one of us to confess.

Everyone remained silent, staring at the top of the table.

"It was my fault," I interjected. "I couldn't control my curiosity and just wanted to see what the woods were all about."

I wasn't even sure what I'd done wrong, but the twist in my gut told me I should have been more patient, particularly since I had no idea what I was really getting into.

Ms. Kelly nodded.

"Thank you, Brynn. But of everyone here, you were the one who knew very little about our code. I would expect the others to share our rules as needed." She glanced around the room.

Courtney kept her head down, and Blake sat comfortably with his hands folded on the table.

Shane lifted his gaze. "You're right," he said to Ms. Kelly. "I got carried away with the mystery as well. I thought Brynn should know more about the history of that place before we got too involved in the project. I lost perspective for a moment." He confessed. "But, I've been corrected now."

"Anyone else?" Ms. Kelly asked.

Dom and Poorva began speaking at the same time, taking responsibility for their involvement in our early explorations, but the sound of their voices blurred into static as I hung on Shane's words.

He had sent a very clear message to me.

And it stung.

Had he still not seen the text message? Or maybe he didn't believe what I told him.

"Perspective is an easy thing to lose," I blurted. "When you're choosing not to see."

My hand threatened to smack across my mouth as I cursed myself for speaking my mind. Why couldn't I just stay quiet?

Shane shot a narrow-eyed glare at me and then looked back to Ms. Kelly as she spoke again.

"Well, today, we'll have a review of our ethics to be sure our group stays safe and concealed within the school and community. It is our secrecy that gives us our strength, and this term's project will rely on it."

After words like loyalty, privacy, and self-control were reinforced, everyone looked to Ms. Kelly in agreement, assuring her that we understood the code and would abide by it for the safety of our group.

She continued. "So, the reason it is important to discuss this today is because of the volatile nature of our project and its connection to our gifts. We need to hone into our skills more than ever for this one and trust our instincts." She looked at each one of us. "We have a really powerful group this year. One that will likely evolve into something even stronger. So, collectively, we must understand each other's strengths and weaknesses."

Dom's gaze shot to me, and Poorva didn't miss it. She lifted her eyes to the ceiling.

"So, today, our activity will be the round table. Everyone will have an opportunity to speak."

Courtney banged her head off the table.

"Again?" Blake complained.

"Every year, our gifts evolve. We need to reconnect with each other to see where we're at," Ms. Kelly explained.

"Fine." He rolled his eyes.

It made sense that Blake was annoyed. He'd been looking forward to X-block as much as the rest of us, and now he had to endure a 'get-to-know-you' exercise that he didn't even need. He knew us all just by tapping into our thoughts. And he didn't hesitate to use his ability at any and all times. I'd already accepted that as his truth.

"It will take five shifts for all of you to connect," Ms. Kelly instructed. "You'll have four minutes for each session. Keep things to a whisper to respect those around you and ignore me. I'll be moving from group to group, observing."

Courtney let out a loud moan.

Ms. Kelly ignored it and added, "You can begin with the person to your right. Connect hands. Then, when the four minutes are up, the person on the left will rise and move to the next student."

She waited for the anxious shifting to settle, then said, "Begin."

## CHAPTER 12

I turned to my right and glanced at Courtney. She hadn't moved a muscle since Ms. Kelly's directive to begin. I inched over to her and pulled my chair closer. I had to get through four minutes with her and prayed I'd survive it.

"Um, hi Courtney," I whispered. "It's me, Brynn."

I hesitated, not knowing what to do since she hadn't shifted even slightly.

I continued, "I know this is awkward, but I'm glad to have a chance to get to know you a little."

I waited. As each second passed, I became more interested in her and didn't want to lose another moment to see what she was all about.

I reached for her hand that clung to the edge of the table. "We're supposed to hold hands," I said. "Do you mind if I just touch yours?"

Her knuckles turned white as she gripped the table harder.

I looked up to Ms. Kelly, not sure what else to do. She nodded, encouraging me to keep trying.

Maybe if I touched her hand gently, she would be able to see that I wasn't a threat—that I was just as lost as anyone else.

I touched one finger to the edge of her hand.

In that instant, a surge of burning anguish trailed up my arm, scorching every nerve. I cried out in pain.

"Ach." The scream escaped my lips before I could stop it.

Courtney's head flew up, and she stared into my eyes. Fire danced in her pupils, and the burning sensation continued to move through my entire body. I was sure I would explode into flames any second.

Her wild stare held mine without blinking, and she grabbed onto both of my hands. I pulled to release from her grip as pain ripped through my body. Uncontrollable shakes jarred me as I fought her hold.

Then, with a jolt, she released me. I stared into her face, panting from the violent assault.

I shot my gaze around the room, and everyone remained focused on their own partners, unaware of what had just occurred.

"You see me now?" Courtney whispered. "This is my existence."

I nodded in silence.

"And I see you." She gave a slight smile through her tormented pain. "You have good in you." She winced. "Maybe *you* can be the one to help me."

My eyes widened as I became lost in her distress. She was a victim of her gift—or her curse. It was like a sick hyper-form of Shane's clairsentience. But instead of *sensing* other people's emotions and feelings, she physically felt them. But whose?

"Time to switch," Ms. Kelly called out.

Disappointment shot through me. I wanted to know more about Courtney and at the same time, wanted to forget what I knew. Her pain was more than I could tolerate for four minutes, and she lived with it every moment of the day.

"I *will* try to help you," I promised her as I stood and moved to Blake.

As I sat down next to him, I looked back at Courtney. Dom settled into the chair next to her and kept his hands in his lap. He just shared the space with her. He knew.

Shit. I probably wasn't supposed to touch her. Nobody told me that rule.

I looked at Ms. Kelly and caught her eye. She smiled at me as if she were pleased.

Maybe she'd sent me to Courtney first on purpose.

"Hello?" Blake chirped, hands extended to me. "Anybody home?"

"Oh, sorry," I faltered, reaching for him. "That was just really..."

Our hands met.

"Weird?" He finished my sentence.

"Yeah," I said. "Really."

He glimpsed at Courtney and then back to me. "She's got it the worst," he said. "Like, she'd be in an asylum if it weren't for Ms. Kelly."

"Seriously?" I choked.

"Yeah, I mean, look at her. If that's not insane, I don't know what is."

"She's in pain," I stated. "It's not her fault." My annoyance rang out in my voice in response to his lack of empathy.

"True," he agreed. "To the point of insanity." Then he looked deeply into my eyes. "You feel bad for her. You want to save her." He huffed. "It's no use. We've all tried."

His bold statements irked me. He was overly confident for a little sophomore, and I didn't want him in my head.

"Don't be so judgy," he taunted. "I don't mean to be a dick."

"Sorry," I said. "You just seem like you don't care and that you're too self-absorbed to be bothered by her. It's annoying."

"Ah, now we're getting somewhere," he said. "See, once people realize I'm telepathic, they just start spewing truth as a way to get me out of their head." He laughed. "It's hilarious."

"No. It's a violation," I shot. "You need to reel it in sometimes. You know, play dumb. Try to fit in."

My blunt words flew out of me because, hell, he'd read them in my thoughts either way. His skill was strong. I'd have to remember that.

"True. I suppose a social correction is needed now and then. I accept." He pressed his lips together in resignation. Then he blinked with curiosity. "Interesting," he murmured. "You can sense things all around you, like ESP. You're a clairvoyant, but you don't know how to use your skill yet. You didn't realize it was unique."

I huffed, feeling exposed as he read me. So much for him taking my social correction.

"But there's more," he added, scrunching his eyebrows together. "Something stronger. Like a purpose." He focused on me. "You need to tap into it, Brynn."

"What is it?" My eyes widened. "How do I tap into it?"

"I'm not sure. It's something new to the group...." His voice was cut short.

"Time to switch," Ms. Kelly interrupted.

The jolt of the transitions was brutal. It was like being woken from a sound sleep with a blasting alarm. Like the bliss of dreaming, I wished I could stay longer with each person.

I stood to move to my next partner and met his anxious, waiting eyes.

Shane.

I stepped over to Shane, and before I even sat down, I said, "Did you see my text?"

"My phone's dead," he stated.

"Well, I wanted you to know that Poorva drove me to school today. Dom met us in the lot. I just didn't want you to think...."

His hand flew up.

"It's okay. Not a big deal."

"No, it *is* a big deal if you think I lied to you," I whispered in a firm voice.

He exhaled loudly.

"Just sit," he said.

I pulled back in shock. He was seriously pissed and didn't want to hear what I had to say. Well, fine. Two could play at that game.

I sat down and reached out for his hands. He rolled his eyes and brought his hands close to mine.

Was he serious? He was going to make *me* take *his* hands.

*Fine.*

I grabbed onto them, and in an instant, a rush of electrified chills ran through me, causing every nerve to tingle. My stomach fluttered, and then a warm sensation flowed through me, calming every muscle.

His eyes closed as his face flushed, the same way mine felt. His palms grew sweaty, and his pulse pounded through his hands, matching mine.

He opened his eyes and pulled his hands away.

"What the hell was that?" I asked, feeling out of breath.

I wasn't sure if I should feel embarrassed or just freaked out. Maybe he had no clue that whatever just happened between us felt to me like the closest thing to an orgasm that one could have while sitting in school fully clothed.

His reddening face told me different.

He'd felt exactly the same thing.

"Um, that was weird," he mumbled.

Then he smirked and reached for my hands again.

I pulled back at first, but then let him take them.

This time, our connection picked up from the warm sensation, and relief washed over me. I wasn't ready for another blast like the first one.

I was curious if anyone had noticed what happened between us, but then I had to wonder if *everyone* felt it when they touched him. Maybe it was normal.

"Sorry I over-reacted," he said.

"Hmm? What?" I mumbled through my bliss.

"About this morning. I know it wasn't your fault." He lifted a shoulder. "I can feel it in you. I didn't mean to jump to conclusions."

His words morphed into soothing sounds of paradise, and I struggled to snap back to reality. But it was a serious challenge to release the intense feelings of when we'd first connected. I was lost in it.

"It's okay," I breathed.

He chuckled.

"Yeah, that was weird," he added, knowing I was still dazed.

I squeezed my eyes shut in hopes of clearing my head before this became too embarrassing.

He pulled my attention back, saying, "So, you know my skill, sensing other people's emotions and feelings, so now it's your turn to share yours with me." He squeezed my hands gently as if trying to draw answers out of me.

"I don't really know yet," I murmured. "I pick up on things around me, like, I sense things. I'm just not sure to what level, though." I paused. "Blake thinks there's more. Like I have something I haven't tapped into yet."

Shane nodded. "He's right. I feel it, too." He glanced at Ms. Kelly. "And so does she."

Ms. Kelly watched us closely with a knowing eye.

I nearly blushed under her steady gaze, sure she knew what just happened between us. But she only smiled and then moved her attention to the next group.

"Time to switch," she said, a moment later.

Shane's grip didn't release, and I looked at him while pulling gently.

"Later," he whispered.

I tugged again as he released my hands.

Later, what? I wondered. Like, see you later? Or later, dude?

I had no clue and took a wobbly step to my next partner.

Dom.

"You patched up the young buck, I see," Dom said, pulling our chairs closer together.

"I guess you could say that," I agreed. Blush threatened to rise onto my face again, so I cleared my mind of Shane.

"Good of you. Poor kid's too sensitive. Literally." He dragged his chair even closer and reached for my hands. "I hate this activity," he whispered. "I feel like it's a waste of time."

"Seriously?" I gasped. "It's killing *me*. I'm exhausted," I chuckled. "There's so much energy coming off everyone, I don't even know what to think."

His thick brows pulled together. "Well, that makes me feel even worse. I don't pick up on any of it. Am I doing something wrong?"

I took his hands with mine and held them for a moment. Heat radiated from them, sending warmth up my arms. Then I glanced up at him.

"You seem like you're holding something back," I said. "I mean, I don't know if that's just something I'm picking up from you normally, or if it's something more."

"And you seem to make it worse," he murmured.

"Worse?" I pulled my hands back.

"I mean, whatever it is inside me, it becomes agitated when you're around." He reached for my hands again.

"Is that bad?" I grimaced.

"I don't know. It doesn't feel bad, but it doesn't feel good either. It's kind of an out-of-control feeling." He glanced back at Shane. "What did you feel when you touched him?"

*Oh, shit.*

"Um, he feels things very strongly, I guess. Like, so much it causes him pain." I hoped Dom already knew that about Shane. I figured he must, so this was safe ground.

"Yeah. He's a pussy." He smirked.

"No." I shook my head. "He's a friggin' warrior."

"Hmff." He shrugged. "What did he feel in you?"

"I'm not sure. And that doesn't matter," I redirected. "We need to pay attention to this." I eye-balled our hands.

He lightened his grip on mine and moved his thumb down the middle of my hand.

"I like how you smell," he said.

"What?" I grabbed the ends of my hair with my other hand and sniffed it.

"No, not your hair products. More just, you." He lifted my hand closer to his face, but I held it from getting too close.

I shot a side glance to Ms. Kelly, wondering if this was getting too weird. Her eyes moved over us and around the room, like nothing unusual was happening.

"I have a heightened sense of smell," he huffed. "It's called clairalience. Ms. Kelly says I can smell things when they filter in from the spirit world. Like messages are channeled to me through scent."

I tugged my hand away from his face.

"Wow. Well, sometimes I smell my grandmother, and she's been gone a long time," I said. "Is it like that?"

He kept hold of my hand.

"That's more like memories being triggered by something unexpected," he said. "Mine is more like I can smell things that are miles away, like a shark to blood. Supposedly, I should be able to learn how to control it more, but for now, it's just a bit bizarre to me." He pressed his lips to the side. "But right now...." He lifted his gaze to me. "I like it."

"Okay, that's just weird," I blurted. "Stop." I bulged my eyes at him for emphasis.

"I'm sorry. I can't help it," he pleaded. "I'm usually sickened by all the scents that overwhelm me. This is the first time, around you, that I've been comfortable."

My shoulders relaxed. Okay, maybe it wasn't a hyper-sexualized thing. Maybe that was just my own twisted spin on it. Sheesh. I needed to get my head out of the gutter.

But then I looked into his eyes, and I swore I saw a hungry wolf. Just like my grandmother always warned me— "Beware of the wolves. They'll hunt you mercilessly." Little did I know at the time, this was the exact scenario she was warning me of.

"Last switch," Ms. Kelly called.

I released Dom's hands and the intense heat left with them. It was clear he bottled a ton of energy within himself, and it escaped from him through the heat he radiated.

Then I turned to Poorva and exhaled with relief. Finally, someone I could relax with.

She smiled too, and we jumped to our seats. We faced each other, knees touching, and held hands immediately. "Holy shit," she whispered. "We have so much to talk about." Her giddy voice made my knees bounce. "Not here, though. Later."

"Definitely," I agreed. "What the fucking fuck? So much just happened."

"I know right," she spat.

Then she sat back for a second and gazed at me.

"Wait," she said, leaning in closer again for a better look at my face. She stared into my eyes, deeper than anyone had ever looked. "You're open," she murmured.

"What?" I pulled my knees together. "What the hell does that mean?"

I blinked, to try to back her off.

She ignored me completely, lost in her revelation.

"Ms. Kelly," Poorva called out. "She's open!"

## CHAPTER 13

Ms. Kelly flew over to us and jumped into Poorva's seat. She took my hands and gazed deeply into my eyes. Before I had time to resist, the bell rang, and everyone jumped up.

"It's alright," Ms. Kelly said to them. "Head to class. I'll send Brynn along in a minute." Then she called to them again. "You can begin your research now. Search for clues within the woods and study them with the steps I taught you. Report back next week with your findings."

They filed past us, hoisting backpacks and staring at my face for any sign of what Poorva might have seen. They surrounded her as they left, hoping to get more information.

Being 'open' sounded like a rather embarrassing predicament, and I dropped my eyes low.

"Look at me," Ms. Kelly instructed. She held my hands with light pressure.

I lifted my gaze to hers.

But instead of feeling violated from her looking into my open soul, I stared straight into hers as well.

The essence within her appeared to me and looked nothing like her. She was older and wiser than her outer appearance. It was as if her body was a disguise or temporary housing for something much more powerful than a mere human.

My eyes widened as I saw her true form for the first time.

And she knew it.

She gasped and pulled away, shooting her eyes in a different direction.

"I'm sorry," I choked. "I didn't mean to."

She panted and steadied herself on the chair. "No, it's okay, Brynn. You didn't do anything wrong." Her brow furrowed as she studied me. It was as if she felt in danger.

"I don't know what happened. I just... I just was able to see," I stammered.

"You've seen more than the others," she said. "Your sight is clear. Poorva was right. You're open now."

"What does that even mean?" I begged.

"It means you're ready. Ready to tap into your full power." She hesitated. "And judging by the way you just looked into my soul, your gift is strong. Stronger than any."

I narrowed my eyes as I studied her longer.

"I don't understand what's happening. Who *are* you?" I asked.

She placed her hands in her lap. "I am an educator. A teacher for the gifted students of this school. And I must hide in this role as the quirky school counselor. It's the perfect disguise, wouldn't you say?"

I nodded, having no idea what she should really look like. Probably a two-hundred-year-old wild woman.

"But why?" I asked. "What's the purpose?"

"It's my duty to the spirit world—to continue the training of the new sensitives. Honing your abilities is what keeps the energy flowing. And it strengthens all of you to become guardians as well."

"Guardians of what?" I cringed, fearing what she would say next.

"Guardians of the mystic," she said. "To keep the darkness away. To block the evil that attempts to creep into our town and our lives every day." She gazed into my eyes again. "And you're ready. Ready to face it."

"No," I said. "No, I'm not."

"Yes, Brynn," she stated. "You are."

"No, I..."

She took my hands again and squeezed them. "Your new friends will help you. They are all very gifted and know how to use their skills well. Stay with them, and you'll be stronger together."

I paused, holding back my resistance.

Thinking of going into the woods terrified me now—especially with a bunch of... well, freaks.

∼

*Ugh.* Dom was right.

We *were* freaks.

I'd always known it to be true. I was a freak.

But now I was being put to the test, to figure out what it was that made me different.

Did I have what it took to embrace what I truly was and be the best version of what I could become? Suddenly, the term freak didn't sound so bad. It was more like another term for powerful.

I'd promised Ms. Kelly I would try, just as I headed to history class. She'd written me a late pass with a few extra minutes added to it, so I took my time, taking the back stairs for the scenic route.

As I entered the quiet stairwell, I startled by movement from the shadows. Shane stepped out from the dark space under the stairs and moved toward me.

"Shit," I gasped. "You scared me. What are you doing here?"

"Waiting for you," he said. "There's no way I could just go to class now. Not after all that," he huffed. "And that's never happened before, like, for Ms. Kelly to sit with someone like that. I need to know what happened in there."

His curiosity was understandable. Even I didn't really know what just happened, but it was clear that it was profound.

"But you're going to be late for class now," I said, wondering how he'd get out of this new dilemma.

He looked at the pass in my hand.

"Let me see that." He grabbed the paper and examined it. "There's room for my name on it, too. And, since we're going to the same place...."

"Here, I have the pen she used." I passed him the blue pen Ms. Kelly had borrowed from me.

He bit his bottom lip as he wrote his name onto the pass, next to mine.

"There. Perfect." He inspected his forgery. "Come on. Let's move. We don't want to get caught messing around in the stairwell." He chuckled.

As we walked, our initial silence made me nervous. I couldn't be sure if he was thinking about when our hands had touched or if he was focusing on what Poorva and Ms. Kelly had discovered about me. He was difficult to read, but it was easy enough to feel his vibe that he wanted to spend more time out of class than in.

"So, that session was kind of intense, right?" he stated. "It's always the most awkward one because we're all sort of exposed to each other, you know."

"Ah, yeah. You could say that," I huffed. "I still have no idea what just happened for the past half hour. My mind is mush after that."

"Well, seems like we have a strong new addition to the club," he said, glancing at me from the corner of his eye.

I took a deep inhale. "Yeah, I suppose."

"You'll get used to it," he added. "Especially when we start our research. That's when you'll come to depend on it." He slowed his pace. "So, what did Ms. Kelly see in you?"

I kept moving, and he caught up. "I'm... I'm not really sure. But she seemed pleased."

I felt bad for not telling him everything, but it didn't feel right to tell anyone about what I saw in Ms. Kelly. It wasn't my place, and it was her privacy. I hoped I was making the right choice.

Shane glared at me, knowing I was holding something from him, and he couldn't stand it.

"Fine, whatever," he exhaled. "Just be sure not to keep it a secret too long. We might need some of it at some point."

As we turned into the history hallway, our classroom door came into view.

"So should we begin tonight?" I whispered.

His eyes brightened, and he nodded as we stepped into the monotone drone of APUSH.

With the idea of starting our research tonight, I couldn't think of anything else. The minutes dragged on like hours as the school day ticked away like it had nowhere else to be.

I'd taken the lengthy torture as an opportunity to plan our visit to the woods. As soon as I could pull my phone out, without the fear of it being taken away, I sent a group text to start the planning. I hoped the others would know what to bring and what time would be best. I also wondered about the steps that Ms. Kelly had referred to—steps to follow when conducting our research.

At the sound of the last bell, I darted out of the school in search of Poorva. As soon as I found her in the crowd of fleeing students, I realized she had been searching for me as well.

"So, did she see anything in you?" Poorva gushed, grabbing onto my wrists. "I've been dying to hear. Come on." She pulled me toward the student lot. "I'll drive you home."

I hesitated at first, looking around for Shane. It was a strange reaction that surprised me. I guessed I just didn't want to abandon him. But with no sign of him anywhere, I followed Poorva gladly.

"I'm not really sure what she saw," I answered, still unsure of how much to share. "It was just... weird." I stopped and looked at her. "I'm actually curious what *you* saw when you said I was open. Like, what does that even mean?"

She squinted her eyes and shook her head, as if to clear it and said, "I don't know for sure, but as soon as I looked into your eyes, it was endless. Like staring into the universe. I can't explain it really, but I felt like if I looked any longer, I'd get lost and never find my way out."

My eyes widened. "Don't say that," I snapped. "You're scaring me."

"Well, it's the only way I can describe it. It was like... like you were open."

I held my breath for a moment then let it flow out. Her words unsettled me. I didn't want to be open. It made me feel like anything could enter and mess with me. Or maybe things could leave—things that maybe I needed. The concept screwed with my head, and I wished that closing my eyes would make it go away. But I knew better. Something had shifted within me, and it was real now.

I rubbed my face.

"It's as if, being around you guys, like, around your energy, somehow made mine come out more." I chewed my lower lip.

"That's what happens," Poorva agreed. "When we're together, our powers intensify. You'll see for the first time tonight if everyone can come. It's gonna be crazy."

∽

Very little was said in the group chat, but it was at least enough for everyone to know what time to meet. Fortunately, Poorva and Shane had been texting me on the side, telling me what to bring and what to expect.

I grabbed my black cinch sack and threw a bottle of water into it, along with my back-up charger and a hoodie.

"Where do you think you're going?" My mother's voice cracked from the living room. "It's a school night."

Her feet poked out from the end of the couch while a throw blanket covered the rest of her. I'd hardly realized she was even there, except for the random snores.

"Studying," I replied. "I met some kids from my AP classes who have a study group. I'm going to give it a try."

"Sounds like a lot of distraction," she mumbled. "Just an excuse to go out on a school night."

Argh. Why did she suddenly care? The one time I really wanted to do something, and she's getting involved.

"I won't be out late," I assured her. "I think it's worth giving it a shot. The classes here are pretty intense."

"I told you you should take easier classes," she said. "Just move down to the regular level. Problem solved."

My eyes closed as I used my inner voice to calm myself.

I chanted, "It's not my fault. I don't deserve this. Hard work will pay off. A good education will take me away from here." These were the words that kept me sane, each and every day.

I fought the other words that threatened to burst out of me, things like, "And did that work out well for you?" or "What? So I can be like you when I'm forty?"

But no. I'd never say such hurtful things to her.

Instead, I protected her. I had no idea why. It was a primal thing, I figured. I'd never let her know how much she'd let me down. It would destroy her.

"Well, it's too late to change now, so I guess I just have to suck it up," I said, praying she would let it go.

Poorva pulled up outside, and I secretly rejoiced that I'd made the plan with her before Shane or Dom made an offer. If a guy picked me up, I'd be done.

"Okay, my ride's here," I said, slinging my cinch sack over my shoulder and opening the door.

She glanced at the floor by my feet. "Aren't you going to take your backpack?" she asked with pinched eyebrows.

*Shit. Fuck.*

"Yeah, thanks." I shook my head as if I'd been absentminded.

I grabbed my pack and flew out the door before she could say another word.

"Go, go, go," I blasted as I jumped into Poorva's car, throwing my pack into the backseat. "My mom's asking questions."

She pulled away as we kept our eyes forward, just in case Mom had followed me out. If she was on the warpath, I'd just have to deal with it when I got home.

There was no way in hell I'd let her stop me now, though. We were about to begin work on our first project and I was nearly jumping out of my skin with excitement. I reached for my phone and turned off my maps, just in case she was savvy enough to track me. Fortunately, she had a second interview in the morning at the DPW. The timing of that distraction was perfect.

"The backpack decoy," Poorva laughed.

"Yup," I huffed. "I nearly forgot it, though. Made her suspicious."

She rolled her eyes.

"The things we need to do to keep them off our trail." She turned and passed the school. "Do you have a full charge?"

I glanced at my phone, and it glowed at ninety-nine percent. "Yup. And my external charger." I patted my cinch sack.

"Good." She glanced at her own phone, plugged into her car charger. "For some reason, our batteries drain really fast when we're all together. We'll need every percentage point we can get."

I considered the idea of running out of a charge while in the middle of the woods—no flashlight, no GPS.

"Um. Like, how fast?" I murmured.

"Fast enough that we won't want to linger too long in the darkness. We just need to get in and out, quickly. Long enough to gather some clues and then bolt." She flew down the road that led to the entrance to the woods.

"That sucks," I choked. "I'm already stressed enough. That adds another layer of panic."

"Totally." She shook her head and pulled into the lot by the trail.

The RAV and black Jeep were parked along the side, and the three guys waited at the benches. Courtney was nowhere to be seen.

Poorva and I grabbed our things and hopped out.

"Courtney's not with you?" Dom called to us, while Shane and Blake watched.

"No," Poorva said. "She's been out of touch. I have no idea what she's doing."

"Shit," he blasted. "You gotta just show up at her house. She's been extra weird with this one..."

Crunching gravel turned all of our heads as a shiny, dark BMW pulled into the lot. Its headlights blinded us as it idled for a moment, checking us out. Then the passenger door opened and closed, leaving us wondering. The Beemer reversed out then, and as the headlights angled away from us, we stared at a dark figure standing motionless in the lot.

As our eyes adjusted, her head lifted.

"Courtney!" Poorva called, running over to her.

Poorva spoke quietly with her for a moment, then the two of them joined the group.

"Hey," Shane said. "We're glad you're here."

Courtney gave a weak smile, causing everyone to smile as well. The energy of the group lifted immediately.

The feeling was different now that all of us were together. It was true. As a team, we were stronger than when we were apart. We'd have to use that benefit to our advantage.

Dom checked the time on his phone. "It's seven-thirty. What's our plan?"

## CHAPTER 14

Shane was the first to move toward the opening of the trail and turned to all of us.

"So, do we go in by team or all together?" he asked.

Oh, right. We were supposed to work in two groups. I hated that. I just wanted to stay as one team.

"I wouldn't mind sticking together for the start of our research," I suggested, praying everyone would agree.

Going into the woods as a group of six sounded much better to me than a smaller group of three.

Without hesitation, everyone agreed to stay together for our initial entry into the forest, and my tense jaw released almost instantly.

"Okay." Shane nodded. "So, we go in, search for anything unusual, and then regroup back here. Don't waste any time in the woods, discussing ideas, or making plans. Save that for when we get back out. Last thing we need is to get distracted in there or lost."

"Agreed," Poorva said.

The rest of us nodded as well.

"So, let's plan on thirty minutes in there," Shane added. "That will give us enough time to look around, and then get out before our batteries die."

"It's exactly seven forty-five," Poorva said. "So, at eight-fifteen, we gather back here."

"Yup," Shane said, then he took a deep breath. "Flashlights on. Let's go."

We entered the trail opening, and I locked arms with Poorva. She gave a nervous chuckle and clamped on tight.

Shane and Dom led the way, and we followed close behind. Blake and Courtney lingered at the rear, sending a false sense of security to me.

Pitch darkness surrounded us as we moved deeper into the forest. Tall tree trunks lined each side of the trail like watchful soldiers. The pines were cleared of any low branches, having their canopies high above us, blocking any light from the rising moon and stars.

I strained to see through the trees into the depth of the woods on either side. Angling my phone's flashlight to the right, I stared into the darkness, wondering what might be lurking behind each thick trunk or in the low shrubs that struggled to survive beneath them.

"You guys kind of know your way around in here, right?" I whispered to Shane and Dom.

"Yeah, we follow this trail to Hell's Gates," Dom said. "Then, it opens up a bit."

"Wait, what?" I spat.

I'd forgotten about Hell's Gates. Shane had mentioned the name once before, but it hadn't come up since.

"What the hell is Hell's Gates," I choked.

Shane looked back at me with a smirk. The light from my phone cast shadows on his face, creating dark circles under his eyes and making his sharp cheekbones even more pronounced. A shine bounced off his bottom lip, distracting me.

"It's just a name it was given a long time ago," he said. "It's part of the urban legend."

"It's the grounds of a burned down orphanage," Dom added. "Supposed to be haunted." He stopped short in his tracks. "What's that?" he shot, flashing his light ahead of us.

I jumped, pressing closer to Poorva, and Dom let out a laugh.

"Jerk," I mumbled.

We moved farther into the woods, and with each passing step, my anxiety grew worse. Something about the woods at night—it was terrifying. Anything could be hiding, waiting for us, like a psycho-killer or some deranged hermit, or worse—something unworldly.

I felt it all around us.

There was something unnatural here.

An uneasy feeling surrounded me like something unsettled lurked within the darkness.

"Do you guys feel that?" I whispered.

Shane slowed his pace, and Dom held back with him.

"Yeah. I thought it was just me," Shane said. "I feel something too."

Blake pulled up close to us, with Courtney by his side.

"Me too. Like there's something else here. Or someone," he said. "Like there's a seventh among us."

"Shit," I gasped. "Don't say that."

"Just follow Ms. Kelly's steps," Poorva said. "Step one, don't run."

"I hate step one," I whined.

"And step two, keep track of every detail," Blake said.

Shane moved along the trail at a steady pace again. "So, we sense something with us," he said. "Let's go a little farther and see what happens."

"I was afraid you'd say that," I huffed.

We moved along the dark trail, and out of the pitch darkness, a gate appeared, blocking our way. Dom and Shane didn't hesitate and climbed over it first.

"What's that for?" I asked, stepping onto the lower rail.

"I think they put it here to stop people from going this way," Dom said. "Everyone just jumps it. Unless you want to go off-trail to get around it. Extra fencing goes both ways, so you'd have to go pretty deep to get around."

Shane held the long metal gate steady as the rest of us hopped over. I'd seen similar gates at farms, dividing cow fields, and thought it seemed out-of-place here. Fortunately, it was easy to get over, but I couldn't help thinking it would be an unfortunate hurdle in the time of panic and running.

As we moved away from the gate into the darkness of the forest, I noticed the disappearance of the shrubs and underbrush. The woods thinned out to pine trunks only, as if the forest floor had died and only the trees remained.

"Why is it so barren now?" I asked, flashing my light to the sides. "All the overgrown brush is gone."

I scanned the dirt ground that had earlier been covered in what looked like wild blueberry bushes and loads of poison ivy. It was just vacant now.

"They say once you get closer to Hell's Gates, everything dies off," Dom said. "The tall trees are the only thing left, and they're stripped of any growth practically up to the tops."

"Oh, great," I murmured, staring into the void of bare tree trunks all around.

I slowed then, sensing an overwhelming presence. Something that cried out, as if in pain—as if trapped in the pillar-maze of the steadfast trees.

Before I could say a word, a heart-stopping shriek ripped through me, shredding my soul to pieces.

We jolted, turning our lights on Courtney and watched in terror as she tore at her hair, screaming, with arms flailing at an unseen enemy.

She screeched as if she were on fire, and before we could get to her, she took off down the trail, whipping her jacket off and hurling it into the trees. We chased after her as our flashlights sent beams scattering all around, adding to the chaos, and raising my level of panic ten-fold.

"Courtney! Stop," Shane shouted. "You'll get lost!"

She continued running down the trail at a frantic pace, tripping and crying out in pain.

Shane yelled back to us. "She's on fire. Burning from the inside out," he called. "Grab your jackets and prepare to smother her," he commanded.

For a moment, Courtney went out of sight into the darkness. We shined our lights forward, searching for any sign of her as we kept running ahead. With my eyes nearly bugging out of my head, I searched into the trees on both sides.

As we raced forward, the black of the forest turned to an ethereal glow. Moonlight cut through the trees, illuminating a clearing up ahead.

"There it is," Dom shouted. "Keep going!"

I stared, wondering what we were heading into, and my eyes locked onto Courtney's dark silhouette.

She stood in the middle of the clearing with her arms stretched out to the sides and her head tipped back. Her body tensed with every silent scream that tore out of her.

Racing across the long grass, we stumbled through the meadow, focusing only on her. Tripping on granite steps buried in moss and pounding on parts of the ground that felt like stone, my mind scrambled to figure out where we could be. Just as we reached her, she fell back into the grass, and we smothered her with our jackets.

She arched her back in resistance to our efforts as her face contorted in agony.

"Courtney. We're here," Poorva whispered. "You'll be okay. Just breathe. Let it pass."

Poorva's calm voice proved she'd seen this before.

I dropped to my knees and inched closer, wondering if I could help in any way. I placed my hand close to Courtney's leg, offering my support. As my hand came within inches of her, it burst into flames, and I watched in horror as my skin turned black, crackling and peeling.

I jumped to my feet, shaking my hand to extinguish the flame, but its strange purple licks only grew higher. My feet tore out from under me as I ran back toward the shelter of the trees. Streams of purple fire trailed behind me, and with every frantic step, I searched for the opening of the trail.

As I reached the edge of the clearing, trees loomed over me as if they'd huddled together to hide the source of my escape. The flames on my hand extinguished, and I gasped at the sudden darkness that crushed down on me.

I sucked in a huge breath, lifting my burned hand close to my face. There was no pain, and I panted in relief, though I was still unsure if I was injured in some way from the assault.

I fumbled for my phone, realizing it was nowhere to be found. I realized I must have dropped it as I ran in panic, and I turned back to see if it was glowing in the grass. I scanned the meadow, noticing immediately that everyone was gone. They'd all scattered. The lights of their phones had disappeared, and I froze alone in my spot as terror coursed through my veins.

My breath moved in and out of me in short, shallow bursts as I scanned the clearing for any movement. Though the moon lit the meadow with a gentle glow, it was still too dark to see any detail.

By instinct, I crouched to my knees and held myself in a tight ball. No matter how much I opened my eyes, I still couldn't see through the darkness.

My head jerked to the side, following the sound of rustling.

Then the snap of a twig.

I held my breath as I waited in terror for whatever approached me.

Without moving a muscle, I remained crouched in the grass, listening with every fiber of my being.

Then another snap.

My breath sucked in, making a gasping sound, and I smacked my hand over my mouth to silence it.

"Brynn?" A whisper moved through the darkness.

My air whooshed out of me in relief as my tense muscles turned to mush.

"Shane?" I whispered back.

The movement grew louder as he hurried over to me.

"Shit, Brynn. Are you okay?"

"Yeah, I think so." I rubbed the back of my hand, searching for any damage.

"Keep your light off," he said. "It's best to stay hidden right now."

"I don't have one. I think I lost my phone," I murmured.

"It's okay. We'll find it. I have mine." He pushed his phone into his jeans pocket.

He huddled down in the grass with me, scanning the open area of the clearing.

"Poorva's still with Courtney in the middle over there." He pointed in their direction. "I'm not sure where Dom and Blake went. They ran off at the same time you did."

I listened for any sign of them.

"Jesus, Brynn," he said. "What the hell happened?" He pressed closer to try to see my hand. "Are you hurt?"

I shook my head. "No, I don't think so." I rubbed my hands together to check, and everything felt normal. "I'm not sure what that was, but it scared the shit out of me."

"Did it burn you?" he asked.

"No, not at all." I lifted my hand and smelled it. "It's fine," I said, but then hesitated.

It wasn't fine. It was far from normal.

My hand had erupted in purple flame, sending me running for my life. But there was no pain, no damage—only a steady hum that continued to course through my body. The vibration awakened my senses to a height I'd never felt before. At first, I assumed it was my adrenalin, but as I sat in the grass, I realized it was more than that.

"Something feels different," I murmured.

My vision became more clear in the darkness, and my hearing piqued at every rustle. But it was my skin that felt it the most. Every little hair prickled at the slightest motion as if picking up on everything that existed around me.

"There's someone else here," I stated. "They want us to find them. To acknowledge their presence."

Shane pulled back from me and went rigid.

"It's like the flame ignited on my hand when they were close," I mumbled. "Like the flame had sensed their closeness."

Shane fumbled in his jeans and pulled his phone out. He turned on the flashlight and beamed it directly on me.

I lifted my hand to block the blinding light.

"What are you doing?" I spat. "Shut it off."

He turned the light off me and aimed it into the woods behind us and then out into the clearing. He was searching for something... or someone.

"Shane," I hissed.

He turned the light off.

"I feel it too," he said. "He's still here, waiting to be found."

## CHAPTER 15

Someone was here in the woods? Waiting to be found? Shane's terrifying words sent chills through me.

"What the hell are you talking about?" I gasped. "Who's waiting to be found?"

I considered the possibilities of the urban legend of Hell's Gates. Could it possibly be real? If there was any truth in the legend at all, then I was screwed.

Sitting here in the deep woods, in the middle of the ghost story that plagued our town, I questioned my sanity for having been so naive. I swore to be more respectful in the future and not mess with things I didn't understand.

I stared at Shane, waiting for him to tell me who he was talking about. Then I heard him take a deep, shaky breath.

"Tommy," he stated.

"Who the hell is Tommy?" I asked, nearly breathless.

I wasn't sure I even wanted to know.

"My friend who went missing seven years ago," he murmured. "I feel his emotions whenever I come here. He's lost and scared." He paused, attempting to hide the sound of his constricting voice. "I hate this place. It tortures me." He dropped his head to his knees.

I froze in silence. Shane was somehow still connected to the boy who went missing.

No one knew if the kid had died from exposure or worse. The wolf population had been growing, and they were known to hunt in packs. I forced my thoughts to halt. The idea of a boy being mauled by wolves was too much to consider. I squeezed my eyes shut at the thought of the suffering of his poor family. Not knowing what became of him must be torture.

"It's part of your grieving," I said, hoping to soothe Shane. "Holding on to the person you loved. Wanting to fix what happened."

He lifted his gaze. "It's more than that, Brynn."

I looked at him, seeing mostly just his shadowy outline, but as I gazed harder, the details of his face became more evident. His eyes glistened with wetness, and his lower lip trembled.

"Tell me," I whispered.

He pulled in a long, deep breath.

"That time Laney and Dom dared me to go into the woods," he started. "I knew I shouldn't have gone. It wasn't right to tempt evil like that. But I went anyway." He paused, collecting his next words. "When I got out of their sight, I slowed and hid behind a big tree, in case they followed. I wanted them to think I'd kept going."

"And what happened then?" I encouraged him to tell more.

"Running between the trees..." He cleared his throat. "Was a little boy. He looked lost and frightened. I called to him to help him find his way out of the woods, and he stopped short, staring at me with a confused gaze." Shane dragged his hands through his hair. "I stepped closer to him and was terrified by what I saw. I stared right into Tommy's face. Only he hadn't aged at all. He was still nine years old, though it had been a couple years since he'd gone missing."

My hand flew to my mouth.

Shane swallowed in an attempt to loosen the tightness in his neck. "I ran, after that. Right out of the woods, past Laney, and smashed right into Dom as they laughed at me." He paused. "I've regretted running ever since. Just like Ms. Kelly's first rule. Tommy needed my help, and I left him there. Alone."

"Shane," I gasped. "It's not your fault. It wasn't real. It's some twisted way the mind deals with grief and loss. You can't let it torture you like that."

My heart broke for him. He'd been carrying that guilt for years, and it must have been eating him alive.

"It's not like I want it to be like this," he snapped. After a slight pause, he added, "I've been working at strengthening my abilities, so I can face this again. So I can find him."

My eyes widened.

Shane had an ulterior motive for our project. A personal connection.

"Does Ms. Kelly know?" I asked.

He nodded. "Yes. She's trying to help. I think this project could be the one to finish it."

*Figures.* The project I show up for has to be the biggest one our group has ever dealt with.

"And do you think Courtney's torture is linked somehow?" I asked.

He blinked slowly and stated, "I'm sure of it."

A voice called out from the darkness, making us both jump.

"Blake?" Dom's voice shattered the silence around us.

"Dude, what the fuck?" Blake's voice squeaked out of the trees. He stumbled out from behind a massive pine and hurried over to Dom. "Where's everyone else?"

"We're over here," Shane called to them.

He stood and reached for my hand, lifting me with him. We moved closer to Dom and Blake, and regrouped.

"I think Poorva's still over there with Courtney," Dom said, glancing at me briefly.

His gaze jumped back to me again as if trying to figure out what had happened—if what he thought he saw was real.

I instinctively dropped my hands to my sides to try to hide them.

Something strange had changed about me, and everyone knew it.

They all saw the same thing—glowing purple fire shooting from my hand. And their initial silence about it told me they hadn't seen anything like it before.

Insecurity washed over me, and I frowned at myself. Typically, my insecurities were around what people thought of me at school or if I'd be outcasted. Now, this new situation rose above all my other concerns, making them seem trivial.

But at the same time, my power was captivating, and there was no way I should be feeling insecure about it. Instead, I should feel empowered and embrace it. But I couldn't help it. Being like everyone else was so deeply engrained in adolescent mentality, it was difficult to break away from its pull. Plus, I'd already invested so much energy trying to convince myself and others that I didn't care, I at least had a head start.

"So, you gonna tell us about that shit?" Dom nudged at me.

Blake chimed in. "Don't be a dick. She hasn't even had a chance to figure it out herself. Give her half-a-minute, anyway." He stared at me, too, anxiously waiting for a reply.

"Well, can't *you* figure it out," Dom said to Blake. "You seem to know what's going on most of the time."

Blake continued to examine me as if trying to use his skill to understand what might have happened.

"It's a manifestation of her power. As if it grew too quickly and exploded out of her," he murmured through deep thought. "Something triggered it. I'm not sure what."

I rubbed my palms together and felt an electric charge that lingered in my hands. It sent heat up my arms, and I extended my hands in front of me to cool them. As I held them out, a gentle purple glow cast off my palms, and my mind lit up with images of the clearing, but from a time long past.

I moved my hands across the clearing, and more pictures entered my head—a wooden structure, almost like an altar, with stone stairs leading up to it. Another architectural feature stood at the far side, with an ornate masonry arch that spanned the length of it. A massive wooden chair sat in the center under the arch, surrounded by several benches.

I coughed in surprise and pulled my hands back into me.

"Shit," Dom hissed. "You're fucking magic."

"No, shit, asshole," Blake spat, staring at me in shock.

Their comments shot me back to the moment.

"Is it weird?" I whispered.

They looked at one another as if searching for the right words—words we all knew would include terms like odd, bizarre, insane...

Shane shook his head. "No," he said. "It's not weird. It's powerful. More powerful than anything we've seen." He stepped closer to me, reaching for my hands. "We've heard of this kind of thing from Ms. Kelly, but we haven't reached the level where we could actually see our gifts. So, yeah, that purple shit is kind of a mindfuck right now."

I lifted my hands to his, and he grasped my fingertips. Then, he reached farther and took my entire hands into his.

"The heat is intense," he said.

"Easy, boy," Dom teased.

Shane ignored him and looked into my eyes. The glow from the other's flashlights made it easier to see each other's features.

He gasped and dropped my hands, stepping back.

"Shit," he said. "This place isn't a burned-down orphanage." He blinked as if trying to see the images from my mind more clearly and then swallowed hard. "It's something else. Like a theater or arena of some kind."

Blake stepped back from us with cautious movement into the vast space of the clearing.

Of everyone in the group, I'd always considered him the most powerful. I mean, his ability to read thoughts, even from a great distance, was mind-blowing. But the more time I'd spent with the others, the more I'd realized they were *all* powerful, each in their own ways.

And now, I'd finally joined their ranks.

And it scared the shit out of me.

And apparently, it scared the shit out of Blake, too.

He'd turned away from us, uncertain what to think of my purple hands, and headed to the middle of the field.

"Come on," Dom said. "Let's get Poorva and Courtney, and get the hell out of here."

We followed after Blake and gathered around the girls. They sat in the grass, cross-legged as if whispering to one another. They looked up at us with tired gazes as we approached.

"You guys good?" Poorva asked with a slight tone of judgment.

She probably thought we ran from Courtney's episode like scared children. There was a good chance she didn't see my purple-flame-hand-situation while she was trying to rescue Courtney from her writhing.

"Yeah, we're good," Shane said. "How are you guys? Courtney?" He leaned in to check on her more closely.

She took a deep breath and nodded at him as if she were improving.

"Alright, let's get out of here then," he said.

Dom tapped on my shoulder. "Lose something?" he asked, handing me my cell phone.

I grabbed it by instinct. "Thank you," I gushed. Holding it tight like a lifeline. "I can't believe you found it."

I swiped my flashlight on and felt every muscle in my body relax from the relief of its glowing light.

"Maybe it'll encourage you to use it a little more," he smirked, and his thick brows lifted, framing his wise-ass expression.

I rubbed the front of my phone on my shirt and shrugged. "I've never been much of a social media user."

His brows lifted higher like he didn't believe me.

"Do we have everything?" Blake asked.

"Right," Poorva added. "Rule number two. Keep track of everything."

"That means all the intangibles, as well," Shane said. "We need to record everything that happened so we can give Ms. Kelly a thorough report."

"Um, can we do that when we are safely back at the cars?" Blake asked.

Shane chuckled. "Yup."

We started walking toward the direction of the trail opening.

"What are the rest of the rules?" I inquired, wondering what else we needed to accomplish before leaving the woods.

Poorva came up next to me and turned her eyes on Courtney. "Step three—believe what you see."

"And the next to last one is—follow your gut," Shane added.

I liked that one. I was pretty good at it.

I'd always listened to my gut, and it rarely, if ever, let me down.

As simple as the rules sounded, I knew they carried significant weight. Knowing to not run at the first sign of fear was a good one. Then, keeping track of every detail, believing it all, and at that point, following your gut, made perfect sense when encountering things of the supernatural.

I wondered what the final rule was as we continued moving toward the part of the clearing where we had entered.

With all our flashlights on, it was easier to get a sense of location and which way to move. I focused on the dark opening to the trail and pointed my body in its exact direction to be sure not to lose sight of it.

"So, what's the last rule?" I asked with growing impatience, not only to hear the rule, but also to get out of these damn woods as quickly as possible.

Just as the final word left my lips, all of our flashlights flickered and then went dead.

Pitch blackness surrounded us.

In terror, everyone froze in their tracks as a harrowing sound of evil cackling surrounded us from all sides of the clearing.

I listened harder, praying the sound might have a reasonable explanation, but it only grew louder and more menacing. It mocked us with its sinister tone, jabbing at us from every direction.

"The last rule?" Blake stammered. "Run!"

## CHAPTER 16

We flew toward the trail as fast as our feet would carry us. Tripping and stumbling on every bump on the ground, we banged into each other, making our escape even harder.

The terrifying cackling filled the space behind us as we raced to get away from it. Whipping my cinch sack off my back, I searched inside while continuing to run. My hands wrapped around my portable charger, and I pulled it out, then plugged it into my phone.

The entrance to the trail enveloped us as we flew into its darkness. We slowed and reached our arms out ahead of us, careful to not smash into the trees.

"Just keep moving forward," Shane said. "If you feel the smoothness of the trail get bumpy, then you're moving off of it."

I pressed the button on my phone, waiting for the charger to bring it back to life. It glowed, and a line on the screen moved from left to right as it powered up.

As soon as it was ready, I turned the flashlight on.

"Awesome," Shane gasped. "Shine it forward onto the trail."

I shot the beam ahead of us, and it illuminated the path a few feet out.

The small amount of light brought huge relief to everyone as their frantic breathing steadied again. The sound of the cackling had died off, leaving us with only the silence of the deep woods. We kept moving forward, searching for the landmark of the gate.

In an instant, everyone's hurrying came to an immediate stop as we stared at a strange shadow in the middle of the trail. We watched as it moved in small, jerking motions. As the form became more clear, I gasped in horror.

It was a little boy.

He stood panting as his wandering eyes search all around him. His focus landed on us, and he held a lost gaze as if begging for us to help him.

A quiet whimper turned my head from the terrifying sight, and I watched Shane crumble to his knees, shaking.

I knew then what we were seeing.

It was Shane's worst nightmare.

His friend, lost seven years ago in these very woods—never found. And Shane carried that burden every day of his life.

I turned back to the young boy and found my voice. It squeaked out of me as I said his name.

"Tommy?"

His head jerked in my direction, and he stared at me with wide, frightened eyes. Then, in a flash, he turned and bolted along the trail toward the shadow of a high triangular structure. And then, he disappeared out of sight as if he'd evaporated.

I reached for Shane's arm, pulling him up, and we raced after the boy.

Poorva's portable charger finally activated her phone as well, and our two light beams bounced in a panicked frenzy.

Out of nowhere, the cattle gate appeared, blocking our way. We scrambled to it, and as we began climbing, it swung on its hinges.

We jumped off in shock.

Someone had unlocked it.

My air rushed out of me in alarm, and I shone my light all around us. With no sign of movement or anyone around, we continued running down the path toward the lot.

"Tommy!" Shane's voice choked out of him.

"Tommy!" I called along with him.

Dom lagged at the back of the group and slowed with every shout of Tommy's name.

Before long, we burst out of the woods into the parking lot. We moved as far away from the darkness of the trees as possible, gathering around the cars.

Looking back, I noticed Shane still standing at the mouth of the trail, and I went after him.

Placing my hand on his shoulder, I said, "It's not him, Shane. It's a sick mind-trick."

He swallowed hard. "But you saw him, too. We all did."

I nodded, wondering if there was some truth in what we saw. It had seemed so real. "It's like he's trapped in there somehow," I murmured.

Shane shot a glance at me as if he'd seen an opportunity.

"I'm going to get him out of there," he stated. "I don't know how. But I'll get him."

I flinched from the crunch of gravel behind us as Dom approached.

His face hung limp, and he was white as a ghost. He shook his head. "I'm sorry, man."

Shane glared at him.

Dom continued. "I didn't believe it before. It didn't seem possible." He took a deep breath. "I'm going to help you find him."

Shane tipped his head at Dom and then nodded with skepticism oozing from his eyes. Without saying a word, he accepted Dom's offer, with the caveat that he still held some responsibility in all of it.

It was clear that Shane would never forgive Dom for exploiting the loss of Tommy. Bullying him into the woods when they were kids, knowing Tommy had been missing, was heartless.

Shane glanced at me, catching my sympathetic stare, and shook his head. Without saying a word, I knew he thought Dom was pathetic, trying to look good in front of me by being a do-gooder. I rubbed my temples, wondering if it was that obvious that I'd fallen for Dom's charm, yet again.

"Come on," Blake called to us. "We gotta get home. It's late."

We walked over to the rest of the group by the cars, knowing we'd come back another time to finish this.

"Rule two. We need to document everything," Poorva said. "Time check."

Blake looked over her shoulder as she checked her phone for the time. "It's gotta be ten, at least." He glanced around at the strange brightness of the late night. "We were stuck in there forever."

My stomach dropped at how late it probably was, and I tried to come up with an excuse for my mother, mainly since my gut told me it was even later than what I'd thought. We'd gone into the woods at seven forty-five and had been in there a lot longer than expected.

Poorva coughed. "Umm, guys."

We gathered around her.

Her eyes narrowed in confusion as she stared at her phone and said, "It's not even eight o'clock yet."

∽

There was no way it could be possible.

We all checked our phones and saw the same thing—seven fifty-nine.

But we'd been in the woods for much longer than fourteen minutes. It felt like at least two hours. So much had happened, between trekking in the dark, Courtney running away and then collapsing, my purple glowing hands, and then hiding from it all at the perimeter of the woods. Our walk back to the car alone was a good twenty minutes and seeing Tommy made it even longer.

"There's no way," I spoke my thoughts out loud, scratching my head.

"It's like a time warp of some kind," Poorva added. "A time-space continuum."

Dom huffed. "Enough of that AP Physics shit. What the hell is happening?"

"It's quantum physics, dumbass," she spat.

"But it's more than that," Shane said, staring into the woods. "It's something supernatural, like a portal."

I thought of the legend of the Dark Witch, remembering the sound of cackling as we ran out of the woods. It resonated deep within me and connected to something I knew well.

"Like witchcraft?" I murmured.

Shane's eyes darted to mine, and his lips pressed together. He didn't say a word or even a nod.

I stared back at him in silence, wondering what the strange sensation in me could be—like an insatiable urge to go after the Dark Witch. To find her. And end her.

"We're sorry, Shane," Poorva whispered. "You know, about Tommy."

Shane lifted his eyes slightly to acknowledge her and then lowered them again to mine.

Courtney paced by the cars, biting her nails.

"We need to get out of here." My heart rate accelerated from the thought of getting dragged back into the woods by whatever force whirled around us. As much as I wanted to go back in there, we weren't ready.

"No shit," Blake said, bouncing in his heels.

"Courtney, come with us," Poorva said. "We'll take you home."

We climbed into the car as the guys went to theirs. Blake climbed in with Shane and slammed his door shut as if fending off a band of attacking ghouls. I was surprised he didn't lose a shoe.

Heavy fog settled in around us as the air grew colder, and I glimpsed behind one more time as Poorva pulled out of the lot. Whirls of mist reached out from the darkness of the trees as if searching for something.

I stared in terror at Dom and Shane, gravel kicking up behind their tires, as the creeping mist nearly reached them. The wind from their moving vehicles sent the curious fog into a whoosh of scattered smoke.

Courtney remained silent in the backseat, rocking in subtle motion, as Poorva and I chattered non-stop about whatever the hell just happened.

"I can't believe we saw Tommy," Poorva gasped. "I don't know how Shane can even function after that. We all knew he struggled with the loss daily, but never did I imagine something like that could happen."

I rubbed my eyes. "How is it even possible that we all saw the same hallucination?"

"It must have something to do with our heightened senses. Like, maybe we were all thinking about him at the same time, and collective consciousness generated the image."

I huffed and shook my head. "I don't know even know what collective consciousness is. But it felt real. Like he was truly there." I hesitated, remembering every moment. "Did you see the look in his eyes? His terror? I'll never forget it."

Poorva kept her eyes on the road, trying to understand what occurred.

Courtney let out a whimper from the backseat, and I shot my head around.

"What, Courtney? Do you know something?" I asked her.

She whimpered again, hiding her face from me.

"You need to tell us," I pressed. "If you know something, tell us."

I wished my voice hadn't taken such a harsh tone because it only made her clam up more. But I couldn't help it. All her silence suddenly became the loudest thing around me.

She had answers. Answers that scared the shit out of her and speaking of them would make it even more terrifying, but I held no mercy. Shane needed my help, and Courtney was the closest thing to it.

Finding Ms. Kelly tomorrow became my primary focus. I planned to tell her everything that happened, including Courtney's episode. And seeing Tommy.

I couldn't wait for the next X-block. I had to get more information now.

Poorva pulled up to Courtney's house, and without a word, she shuffled out the back and hurried inside. The door slammed shut without her even giving a glance back.

"She'll only shut down if you push her like that," Poorva said.

"I don't give a shit," I shot back. "That girl is the center of all of this somehow. Didn't you see what happened to her in the middle of that field? It was like she was being sacrificed or some fucking shit." I exhaled. "Ms. Kelly's protecting her, and it's time we figured out what they're hiding."

Poorva sighed and shook her head. I could tell she thought I was getting ahead of myself—ahead of all of us, running half-cocked. But seriously, I'd seen enough tonight to prove that something was very wrong here.

There was something evil in Lakefield. And it had controlled the people of this town for long enough.

∽

I closed the front door behind me without the slightest sound and took my first step toward my room.

"That was fast." My mother's voice hit me in the back of the head. "You can't expect to graduate with honors with willy-nilly study habits."

My eyes closed in an attempt to settle my temper. Attacking my study habits was so far removed from reality. I was a straight-A student, and she had no idea the effort I put into my studies every night. It was infuriating.

"Yeah, well, senior slump might be hitting early," I snarked.

"No matter," she called to me as I moved down the hall. "We never last long enough in one place for it to even make a difference."

I closed my door behind me in hopes that cutting off her words would keep them from ever coming true. How she could be so heartless was beyond me. Didn't she realize that dragging me around from place to place had created deep insecurity in me, causing fear of attachment, and all the other psycho-bullshit I'd read about in AP Psych?

But this was the first time it ever *really* mattered.

I couldn't leave now. There was too much to do. Too much at stake.

For Shane. For Courtney.

I thought about the vision of the little boy in the woods and sensed his presence all around me.

He was real.

I felt him. Everywhere.

For Tommy.

I had to save Tommy.

# CHAPTER 17

The following morning, I fast-walked through the corridors to get to my English class. I'd barely slept after the woods and felt like my eyes were bugging out from my anxiety.

No one was responding to my texts or Snaps. It was as if all communication had halted. So, seeing the other UMAs was my primary focus, and having a chance to talk with Ms. Kelly was right up there as well.

I swerved some freshmen and cut hard into my classroom. Without any UMA sightings yet, seeing Dom was a priority. He seemed to have a lot of information about Tommy and had promised Shane he would help. It was high time I got some details, and if I pressed Dom enough, I was sure he'd spill.

He hovered over his desk, dropping his pack by his feet like it weighed a ton. His broad shoulders filled the aisle, and I wondered how public schools had the gall to keep full-grown young adults under their control to this point. We should have been released from this prison a year ago, at least.

I shot up his aisle, but before making it two feet, Laney blocked my way.

"What the actual fuck?" she snarled in my ear.

I recoiled from her attack, searching my mind for any offense against her.

She lashed out again and under her breath, said, "Was I unclear?" She pressed her shoulder into me. "You're traipsing where you don't belong." Her eyes glanced at Dom and then back at me. "I won't play nice anymore, you bitch. It's time I made this very uncomfortable for you."

Was she still talking about Dom?

"Laney, you have nothing to worry about," I stated.

I mean, sure, Dom was hot, but nothing was happening between us—that I knew of, anyway. I guess it could. But it wasn't.

I cringed at my incessant inner monologue.

It was official. I *was* cringy.

Like a typical teen, I couldn't get my head straight around how I felt about a guy.

We had chemistry—that was obvious. But something was getting in between us. Distracting me. And it wasn't Laney.

Oh, right, Laney.

She was still in my face, seething.

"Seriously," I added. "I'm not going after your guy."

There. I said it.

She leaned in even closer, and I could feel her breath on my lips.

"Stay away from him," she sneered. "And stay away from the woods. You have no idea what you're messing with."

My breath stopped short.

*The woods?*

Something about the woods had her all riled up. What the hell?

I stared at her as she slipped back to her desk and into her chair.

Dom turned and stared with an expression like he'd just missed something.

And he had.

I lifted my brows at him and pressed past to my seat. Dropping down into my chair, I caught him continuing to stare at me, and I shook my head to try to get him to stop.

He glanced back at Laney then and caught her death-stare.

Lowering himself into his chair, he knew something was up.

Then his text lit up my phone.

*WTF was that*

I concealed my phone under my desk and tried to type without lowering my eyes too much. Mr. Benson had entered the room, and he was stealth at detecting illegal phone use.

*L knows about the woods*

I waited for my phone to vibrate again on my lap with Dom's reply.

I waited a bit more.

But he didn't text back.

At the bell, Laney bolted out the door, avoiding me altogether, or so I'd thought.

Dom kept his head down and left without a word.

How could she have so much power over him? It was mind-boggling.

Sure, she was intimidating as fuck. But only in the realm of the hierarchy of high school. Dom needed to get over it and grow a pair.

Baffled, I walked to physics, and as soon as I lifted my gaze, I saw Laney again. This time, she pressed her scowl into Poorva's face.

I couldn't hear what she was hissing at her, but I didn't need to. It was the same assault she had unleashed on me an hour earlier.

My guess was that she'd get to each of us by the end of the day.

Creating insecurity.

Tearing us down.

Divided we fall.

As the day went on, I realized my theory was correct.

The UMAs avoided each other at all cost, proving they'd all been threatened in one way or another.

I counted the minutes to the last bell so I could finally take some action.

I just needed to get to Ms. Kelly.

Before Laney did.

The idea of Laney talking to Ms. Kelly made my blood boil but also sent a sick fear through my veins. The kind where you feel powerless and vulnerable. I prayed she didn't have any power over Ms. Kelly.

As the final bell rang, I sprang out of my seat and raced for the guidance office. The halls were a blur, full of students making their long-awaited exit, and I kept my head down, focused on my sole destination.

I stormed into the main office, and the grumpy secretary acted like I wasn't even there. I waited, out of breath, for her to lift her eyes off her keyboard.

Two seconds later, I lost it.

"I need to see Ms. Kelly," I stated. "It's urgent."

Her fingers paused on the keys, and then she glanced up at me.

"I'll be with you in a minute." Then her eyes dropped back down.

My teeth clenched together instantly.

Without hesitation, I moved past Maleficent and shot toward Ms. Kelly's office.

"She's not there," she called to me.

I stopped in my tracks.

"Why didn't you just tell me that to begin with?" I spat.

"Return to the waiting area where students belong." She pointed back to the space in front of her desk.

*Shit. I was about to lose it on her.*

I stormed past her and bombed straight out the door.

My breath heaved out of me as I trekked in the direction of home. I'd never felt more helpless as I marched toward my house without having accomplished anything in the day.

Losing my mind was the only thing left on the agenda now that the UMAs had fallen silent, and Ms. Kelly was nowhere to be found.

In my frazzled state, I stopped short on the sidewalk and stared at the old white church with the enormous black doors. It belonged on a historic New England postcard, but that wasn't what had caught my attention at that moment.

It was Shane's car in the lot again.

And there was another one next to it this time.

My heart nearly burst out of my chest as I ran across the road toward the church. Jumping the granite steps two at a time, I opened one of the doors and flew into the lobby area. The door closed behind me with an echoing boom, and then silence hovered all around me.

I swallowed, then walked toward the assembly area that housed the pews and the altar. I glanced into the dark space, and my eyes fell on three figures, huddled and whispering at the front.

I stared in disbelief as they turned to me with half-expectant expressions.

Shane.

The minister.

And Ms. Kelly.

∼

But something was wrong.

The three of them appeared to be calm, but something very intense surrounded them.

I sensed disturbance all around me. Unsettled emotions poured off Ms. Kelly, igniting visions in my mind like the reels of a movie. Flashes of the woods. Fire dancing in Courtney's pupils. And then Ms. Kelly's pain. Not like physical pain of burning or being cut. But more like a deep aching pain. A broken, empty hurt that consumed her from the inside out.

I bent over, clamping my stomach to hold it from bottoming out. A deep moan of sorrow threatened to escape my throat as I willed her pain away.

"Brynn?" Her voice bounced through the church.

In that moment, my mind cleared, and the torment dissipated.

"Ms. Kelly?" I whimpered.

"Brynn, please, come in to us," she called.

I froze, not knowing what to do. I hadn't expected to see her there and wasn't even sure why I had entered the church in the first place.

I should have just let Shane have his meeting time with the minister, without interrupting them. But something had called to my inner soul—something I couldn't ignore.

Shane ran up the aisle and pressed in next to me. "Are you okay? You look hurt." He reached for my shoulder to steady my swaying.

"No, I'm okay. I just got a really strange feeling," I said, shaking my head. "It's gone now."

"Good." He nodded, checking me one final time. "I can't believe you're here. I mean... your timing. It's really good." He led me down the aisle toward the others.

"How so?" I mumbled, still twitching from the strange emotional assault.

He shrugged. "I don't know. Just seems right."

We stepped in front of the alter, and I glanced at the tapestry which was draped across it. An effigy of the mocking of Christ was depicted in its intricate stitching. I withered from the disturbing image of his suffering.

"Hello Brynn," Ms. Kelly said, stepping closer—her voice comforting me like warm honey. "I'm glad you're here. There's been quite a bit going on. Shane told me everything."

I nodded my head. "That's good. I tried to find you after school, but you were already gone."

She smiled gently, as if too weak to do more. "Well, I'm glad you found us now." She turned to the minister. "Brynn, I'd like you to meet somebody very important to me. He's heard a lot about you. This is my husband, Michael."

My eyes widened without my permission. I couldn't hide my surprise no matter how I tried

"Oh," I stammered. "Nice to meet you." I reached out my hand to shake his. Looking back to Ms. Kelly, I faltered, "I didn't realize you could... you know..." I tripped over my words, too confused to make any comprehendible sounds.

"It's okay," Shane laughed. "He's not a Catholic priest. Ministers of this church can marry and have families," he said.

"Oh." I huffed. "Got it."

Ms. Kelly chuckled and turned to her husband. "Michael, Brynn's the gifted one I've been telling you about. I really think she can help."

He gave her a slow nod. "Shane's been keeping me informed on her progress. She may be exactly what we've been waiting for."

*Okay, what was going on?*

*They were talking about me like I wasn't even there.*

"Um, could someone please clue me in a little," I said. "What's going on?"

Shane looked at Ms. Kelly, and she nodded to him, as if giving him permission.

He intertwined his arm into mine and tugged me up the aisle. "Come on. We can talk outside."

I turned back to see Ms. Kelly one more time. Her eyes had filled with tears, and she moved closer to Michael. He reached his arm around her shoulder, pulling her close, and I could swear his eyes glistened too. He watched me with narrowed lids as if studying me with skepticism. His reservation proved he wasn't so sure about me yet.

I whispered to Shane, "What the hell is going on?"

He took a long, slow inhale. "Hell. That's what's going on."

He opened the black oak door, and we stepped out onto the granite stairs. He sat on the top step, and I joined him.

"I don't get it. What's wrong with Ms. Kelly?" I asked. "Is she in trouble?"

I balled my fists, wondering if Laney had anything to do with this.

"She knows we went to the woods last night," Shane started. "This is the project we've all been training for. It means a lot to all of us."

"I know," I said. "It's important to me too. Every bone in my body knows I was meant to be a part of this. I'm just not sure why."

He stared out at the road, watching cars zoom by. "We know. Ever since you arrived, we've all felt more energy, more focus. Like you were the missing piece. It's almost like you awakened something in this town that had been sleeping for a very long time."

His words confused me.

"You're starting to freak me out a little," I interrupted.

"It's Tommy," Shane said, lowering his gaze to his knees. "We haven't seen him in years. And for him to just show up last night. It was unbelievable. We thought he was gone forever."

I ran my hands through my hair. "I don't understand. I thought he *was* gone. We just saw some crazy mind trick. Collective consciousness hocus-pocus. Right?"

Shane shook his head. "We thought so, too. But now, seeing him again. We know he's still out there. We can feel him more than ever."

A chill ran through me, causing my arm hairs to stand up.

"What?" My voice shook out of me.

"We've never given up hope." He glanced back at the big black doors. "Tommy was my best friend. Getting him back has been my life mission."

"And they're helping you?" I looked up at the church doors, knowing Ms. Kelly and Michael were still inside.

"No. I'm helping *them*," he stated.

I hesitated, staring at him. He'd completely lost me now.

"But why?" I whispered, frightened by the sound of my own voice.

Shane cleared his constricted throat. "Because Tommy was their son." He coughed. "He *is* their son."

## CHAPTER 18

The insidious fear that coursed through me was deep-seeded and powerful. It wasn't the kind of fear that triggered fight or flight. It was more like a feeling of doom that poisoned my insides. It was the worst kind.

After detonating the bomb about Tommy, Shane walked me home, knowing I needed air and space.

"Sorry to blow your mind like that," he said. "I know it must all sound crazy. But this is the truth behind our project."

I closed my eyes for a second to clear my mind.

"I just can't believe they are the parents," I said. "Their heartache must be unbearable."

"The only thing that has kept them going is the fact that I can still sense him," he said. "His essence is still all around us. We just need to find him and bring him back."

I wondered how anyone could hold onto hope for so long. Seven years. With no proof. No evidence. Only hope.

Shane's conviction was impressive. He'd helped the Kelly's through his powerful gift of perception. He'd been able to feel Tommy, but now, he saw him again, for the first time since the dare at the woods. The light in Shane's eyes proved he believed he was getting closer.

Our deliberately slow pace delivered me to my house, much to my chagrin. I wanted more time with him, but I knew he needed to get back to the Kelly's.

Shane left me at my door once he was sure I was ready to go inside. I watched him from the stoop as he walked back toward the direction of the church and felt a twang of loneliness.

Sitting alone in my room wasn't the worst thing I could think of to do. My mind was a scrambled mess, and I just needed to sit on my bed and process the multiple layers of this situation. But still, I couldn't help missing his company.

Stepping inside, I cringed as my mother accosted me.

"I've been waiting for you to get home," she barked. "What kept you?"

Hoping for a quick escape from the impending assault, I said, "I stayed after with a study group for one of my classes. We have a big test coming up."

"Oh." She blinked and stood up from the couch. "Well, I have some news."

My heart stopped.

It always started with that sentence.

Every time, she would act like it was good news and that I should be excited. Then she would crush my world with the plans to move again—either for a better house, a better town, or more job opportunities that she would never pursue.

"What is it?" I murmured.

Her face twisted in annoyance. "Well, first, I got a call from the DPW that I'd benn hired."

My eyes brightened. "Really? That's amazing."

"Yeah, it was," she said. "I haven't had that feeling in a long time." Then she balled her fists. "But then a second call came in. Apparently, someone sandbagged me to the boss, telling him lies about a non-existent criminal record. They say they can't hire me now."

My shoulders sank as my world imploded.

Mom was not good at rebounding. She excelled at avoidance and running away from her problems.

This was the first warning sign that we wouldn't be long in this town.

"So, what are you going to do?" I asked.

"I don't know," she murmured as she crashed back down on the sofa. Reaching for the remote, she took on her glazed expression, staring at the TV, and went silent.

This was the point where I typically started packing.

But not this time.

I had no intention of letting this derail me.

I believed Lakefield was where I belonged. I'd never felt more connected to a place in my entire life.

But I didn't want to believe that.

Believing only made me more vulnerable. It raised the stakes on what I had to lose.

But I couldn't help it. There was hope here in this town, and I latched onto it like oxygen.

Heading to my room, I felt an unfamiliar sense of stability beneath me. It empowered my soul and gave me courage to dive headfirst into my project without reservation.

It was exactly what I had needed.

I wasn't going to allow Mom's mess to change my destiny. It was time I took control of it.

I quickly planned out how I would spend the rest of the evening and the following days, researching supernatural occurrences and psychic abilities, until there was nothing else to find on the topics. I knew I'd be distracted by the worry of Mom's predicament, but for once, I'd push those feelings aside, knowing I had something bigger to focus on.

At this point, I was sure everyone in school would continue to lay low, avoiding contact, so that would allow time for me to practice my sensing abilities.

Maybe at some point, my skills would be able to help my mother. I could only hope.

Little did I know, though, the distraction of my unstable world would riddle me with the disappointment of performance anxiety, creating a block that wouldn't budge.

∽

No matter how hard I had tried, I couldn't get the purple glow to reappear in my hands. Although, I still felt the tingle of the power within me. I continued to practice any chance I got, but frustration seemed to be my only result.

I was sure I needed to be around the other UMAs to get it fully operational and the next X-block was still a few days away. Patience was proving to run thin as I continued to be distracted by my mother's issues and I waited painstakingly to be able to see the UMAs again.

Finally, several days later, advisory period rolled around, and I couldn't wait to get there.

The UMAs had remained silent for days, avoiding Laney's tight scrutiny—clearly threatened by her for reasons unknown. But I was determined to finally get some answers now that we could officially gather together again.

I held my breath waiting for the bell that would trigger my launch to the guidance suite.

The trill of the bell sent adrenalin coursing through me, and I shot through the halls toward my destination. Poorva followed close on my heels, but just far enough away to avoid any unwanted scrutiny.

Rounding the corner by the main office, I bumped directly into a solid blockade.

Shaking off the shock of it, I focused on her stern face.

Laney.

"Someone's enthusiastic about getting to their X-block," she seethed.

"Look out, Laney," I shot, trying to get around her.

"Not so fast," she whispered. "You need to slow down to actually absorb what's happening around you."

Her words sent unease through me. "Huh? What are you talking about?"

She smirked. "You'll see. Maybe you'll finally learn your lesson and back off." She stepped to the side and walked away from me, swooshing her hair over her shoulder.

My stomach clamped into a knot of anxiety, and I hated her for ruining my elated mood. Now I headed toward my advisory group with apprehension and fear.

Damn it. What was her deal? She had a sick need to ruin everyone's day.

I tried to brush off the encounter, but my mind raced with thoughts of whatever it was she was up to. Maybe she'd spread some lies on social media to try to destroy me. Maybe she'd talked to Dom and twisted his thinking. None of it seemed bad enough to match the sinister look in her eye.

She'd done something worse. Far worse.

Entering the guidance suite, I went straight for the conference room.

Everyone was there, including Ms. Kelly, and I relaxed in the knowledge that I wasn't the only one who had raced to X-block.

I closed the door behind me, and in the same instant of it clicking shut, the energy in the room ignited.

Poorva's voice rose above the others at first. "Laney's at it again," she called out. "She cornered Brynn just now, and she's got us all in hiding."

"She's threatening to out us," Shane added. "Like she knows way too much about who we are."

Dom stood. "Jesus. I thought it was just me," he spat. "What the hell is she doing?"

Ms. Kelly pressed her hands in the air to calm us, and Dom sat down.

"We've entered a volatile level of our project," she said. "We're making progress, and it's causing a rift to those around us."

"That means we're doing something right," Poorva announced.

"True," Ms. Kelly agreed. "It means we're making considerable progress." She smiled at us. "I'm impressed with your teamwork. Together, you are very strong. Shane has shared the most recent report with me." She glanced at each of us. "It's time now that you work in the groups I originally structured. The six of you combined are generating too much mixed energy. If you break into teams, you will find much more control over your abilities."

Blake dropped his head back. "It seems safer when we're all together."

Ms. Kelly nodded. "Yes. It would seem. But the energy gets gnarled and tangled, creating chaos instead of focus."

I considered her words. It seemed like she may have had a good point.

When we had been all together in the woods, hysteria and panic resulted when things got too intense. We became caught up in the same situation with no one to turn to. If we were split into two groups, we'd remain more clear in our senses and would have the other team to turn to for help in a time of panic.

"Makes sense," I said. "Being in two teams doesn't mean we're not still working together."

"Exactly," she agreed. "So, have you generated a plan for next steps?" She searched our faces for details.

Shane turned to us. "Our focus has become clear," he said.

We all nodded in agreement.

It was clear that our mission was to save Tommy. And everyone knew we'd made a significant leap toward it becoming possible.

We'd made some form of contact with him. And now we needed to figure out how to cross him back over to our realm of existence—pulling him out of his strange limbo.

Ms. Kelly surveyed the room. "Okay. I feel like things have moved much more quickly than anticipated, and I need to ensure the safety of everyone in this room."

"We're fine, Ms. Kelly," Shane interrupted. "We'll use everything you've taught us, and we'll end this."

Everyone chimed in with agreement and assurance that we would be fine. I wasn't sure how long everyone knew about Tommy being

Ms. Kelly's son, but it seemed like they'd always known. It was an unspoken situation that was now our primary focus.

"I don't know," she said. "I just never expected it to get this far. I knew you all had it in you. I just didn't know you'd mature in your abilities so quickly."

Maybe I was feeling insecure, but I was pretty sure all eyes moved to me at that moment.

I blinked back at everyone.

"Once Brynn was added to the group, everything shifted," Blake blurted.

Courtney lifted her head slightly and glimpsed at me through clumps of messy hair.

Ms. Kelly let out a loud exhale. "Well, I think we need more time to practice skills and to discuss safety measures and..."

Dom interjected, "Ms. Kelly, we'll be fine. We got this."

She smiled and lowered her eyes. A moment later, she whispered through a tight throat, "Thank you."

With only a few minutes left in X-block, I wanted to be sure we knew what our specific plan was for completing our project.

I knew it included going back to the woods, this time with a focused mission of finding Tommy and freeing him. But we had the other situation of the Dark Witch. It was an urban legend, I knew, but it was clear she was connected to Tommy's disappearance and all the other strange happenings in the woods over the years.

She was more than a legend.

And I was certain that freeing Tommy would involve pissing her off.

As I prepared to voice the strategy I'd been working on, the door to the conference room pushed open.

Principal Haney filled the doorway with her over-bearing presence, and she addressed Ms. Kelly in a stoic tone.

"Please come with me, Ms. Kelly," she stated. "Ms. Damien will mind your students until the bell."

I stared at Maleficent as she entered the room with a smug grin. Her short, spiky haircut bristled with anticipation.

Ms. Kelly's complexion turned white as she gathered her things and followed Principal Haney out of the room.

We all stared at each other in confusion. All of our senses were tweaking, and the nervous energy bounced off the walls.

Ms. Damien sat at the head of the table and glanced at each one of us with a judging scowl.

We ignored her, knowing how much she hated kids and her miserable job. Her reputation as the evil front office secretary was known throughout the school, and everyone avoided her like the plague.

Instead, we focused on one another as our senses piqued to a new level of panic. Our concern for Ms. Kelly pushed our thoughts to a concentrated point at the center of the ceiling. We looked up at the same spot, and as we fixed our gazes on it, all our voices exploded in our minds.

Each voice could be easily recognized as everyone called out with the same concerns.

"What's happening to Ms. Kelly?" Blake panicked.

"They know something," Dom repeated again and again.

"Shit. If they go after her, what will we do?" Poorva worried.

"It's got to be Laney. She has to be behind this," Shane thought.

My thoughts centered around the same concerns, and the one that rose to the top for everyone to hear was, "Someone wants us stopped."

As my thoughts became clear to the others, Courtney's voice rose above all, surprising us with its clarity.

"We're on our own now," she stated. "Time to fight."

## CHAPTER 19

Shane caught up to me in the hall after the final bell of the day. I was barreling straight for the main office to find Ms. Kelly, and clearly, I wasn't the only one.

Shane and I smacked into the other UMAs as we closed in on the guidance suite. We'd all had the same idea; enter the office area from the back to avoid Maleficent.

We crept into the suite like mice afraid of waking the cat. As we surveyed the area, Ms. Kelly bumped into the side of her office door with a big cardboard box. Her desk plant stuck out of the top, sending a very clear message to us.

"What the hell?" Dom blurted

Ms. Kelly looked over with an embarrassed expression. "Oh." She glanced through the office area to be sure no one else was around and then came over to us. She placed the box on one of the tables.

"I can help you with that," Dom said, reaching for it.

She smiled as deep sadness shone from her eyes.

"Thank you, Dom," she said. "Thank you all. You've been the most incredible students I've ever worked with. You have no idea of your amazing potential. I only wish I had more time with you."

"What?" Shane spat. "Where are you going?"

She rubbed the side of her face. "They've asked for my resignation," she started. "For 'actions unbecoming of a guidance counselor,' they said."

"What the hell does that mean?" Shane erupted.

She exhaled slowly. "Someone reported me for assigning a project that required unchaperoned research, placing my students in an unsafe situation." Her eyes fell. "I suppose the accusation wasn't far off the mark."

"But this is different," I said. "We're different. Of course we had to do research on our own. That's the whole point of developing our skills."

She shook her head. "No. I let it go too far."

"No, Ms. Kelly," Dom interjected. "You did the right thing for us. You always have. You never send us on our projects unless you know we can handle them. This time is no different. We can handle this."

"He's right," Shane agreed. "We can do this, Ms. Kelly. And without you, we would never have believed we could."

Her guilt permeated the space between us, and it killed me. I meant it when I said we were different. School rules didn't quite apply to us in the same way as everyone else. I mean, how else would we grow and learn about our gifts if she didn't push us.

But from the perspective of the school, I could see the problem. Administration had no clue about what we were really all about, and it had to stay that way. I just couldn't believe someone ratted out Ms. Kelly. She was the most amazing person in the entire school. She taught us real-world skills, not just textbook rhetoric.

Then my mind jumped to the whistle-blower, and my fists clenched with white knuckles.

I looked at Ms. Kelly. "Laney?" I asked.

Her lips pressed together. "Mrs. Rosco," she stated.

Laney's mother? What business did she have getting involved in this?

Shane's head nodded in micro-beats like he knew exactly what that meant.

Ms. Kelly went on, "She's always had it out for me. You know, there are always going to be haters. Unfortunately, this time, one of them was able to win."

Staring at Ms. Kelly, I wondered what power Mrs. Rosco could have over her. And then, the sound of a commanding voice made me jump.

"Please give Ms. Kelly some space, students," Principal Haney barked. "I'm sure she'd appreciate some privacy right now."

She ushered us out of the guidance suite like sheep. All we could do was look back at Ms. Kelly one final time.

As our emotions ran to their highest level, our voices burst loud and clear in my mind again.

Shane's voice rang out most of all as he called to her. "Ms. Kelly, we'll finish this. We promise. Stay with us, please."

His words brought tears to my eyes as we all followed his lead and begged her to stay with us.

Then, to my immense surprise, a new voice entered our collective consciousness.

And it was hers.

"Thank you, students. I will not leave you. I will always be your mentor."

And then Principal Haney slammed the office door, leaving us standing alone in the hallway.

There was a cost to using our magic—a price to be paid, and the cost was Ms. Kelly, our mentor.

Losing access to her in school was a deep blow that left us feeling fragmented. We stumbled down the hall as if our bones were broken, and all support removed. By the time we made it outside, we were breathless.

Shane spoke up first.

"She would want us to finish the project," he said. "We need to keep going as if nothing has changed. She might be out of the school, but she's still our teacher."

My eyes brightened, and I nodded at his words.

Then another voice shot into our group from the side of the stairs. "You don't know when to stop?" Laney chided. "It's over."

Dom stood taller and stepped closer to her. "You did this?" he accused. "Why?"

Laney shrugged with a smirk. "Protecting my own interests," she said and then walked away with her chin up.

Blake shook his head. "Bitch," he whispered.

"Who does she even think she is?" Poorva hissed. "She has no idea what she's messing with."

Shane shook his head. "She seems to know more than we realize, and is willing to do anything to stop us." He watched her disappear into the student lot. "She's dangerous and we can't forget that."

Dom continued to posture in Laney's direction, breath heaving out of him. Heat radiated off his skin as his anger mounted.

"Stay cool, Dom," Shane said. "She's not worth it. Don't let her set you off."

Dom exhaled, releasing his shoulders from his ears.

Shane added, "You need to keep a handle on that temper, especially here."

Dom shook his head in agreement, and I watched a line of sweat trickle down from his brow.

He was holding in a serious amount of energy, and it only seemed to be growing. I wondered what he was truly capable of and was pretty sure he was wondering the same thing.

Shane stepped into the middle of our group. "So, we're starting to understand what our skills *can* do. What's starting to bother me, though, is what they *can't* do." He pressed his lips together. "With all of our abilities combined, we still can't rescue Ms. Kelly."

I took in a deep breath. "Or maybe we can," I said.

I was sure there was a way to redeem her. If we just continued to follow our plan and complete the project, it might shed light on why Ms. Kelly did what she did. And maybe she'd be pardoned.

"If we finish this, we might be able to prove that Ms. Kelly was helping us and doing the right thing all along," I added.

"Fat chance," Blake snarled. "School committee's got its rules."

"Well, if we can at least expose Laney with her ulterior motives, it could shed new light on Ms. Kelly's situation." I waited for everyone to think about it.

Shane spoke up first. "Seems like we're all in agreement to keep moving forward with our project, so it can't hurt to try to uncover the motives behind the accusations."

"Exactly," I added.

Everyone agreed, and without another word, we disbanded as if it was just another ordinary day.

But of course, it was far from ordinary.

It was a pivotal turning point for all of us.

And the turning point had just sent us in the direction of no return.

Lost in thought, I trudged toward home with the weight of my backpack bearing down on me. I hated not being able to meet with the UMAs out in the open. It was so difficult to process everything when we had to remain secretive and in hiding all the time.

I just wanted a chance to keep talking and planning. The frustration of it all was enough to make me crazy.

As if my prayers had been answered, a car rolled up behind me, and as the window rolled down, a friendly voice called out.

"Hey, get in," Shane yelled, leaving no room for negotiation.

Without hesitation, I jumped in.

"Hi," I said breathless. "Where's everyone else?"

"Spreading out for a bit. Who knows who's watching us at this point," he said. "Best to be safe."

He pulled out into traffic, and we drove past the church and then past my house.

"Where are we going?" I asked.

"I don't know," he said. "Anywhere away from all this shit. Somewhere we can breathe."

I smiled in agreement. "Sounds good."

I texted my mother that I'd be running late—staying after school.

"I can feel the intensity of this place lift as I drive further away from town," he said. "Do you feel it?"

He was absolutely right. The heavy weight on my soul lightened with each passing mile, and my mind cleared to the point where I could think right again.

"Yeah, I feel it," I sighed. "It's good."

"I like to think it will feel like this all the time once we finish the project," he said.

"That would be amazing. Do you think it's possible?"

He shrugged. "We have to hope so. For Ms. Kelly's sake, especially."

I thought of Ms. Kelly and the pain she was enduring. Losing her son was by far the worst torture a mother could ever face, and now, losing us... it could crush her.

"Do you think we'll be able to find him?" I whispered.

Shane turned his gaze on me for a moment, then back onto the road.

"Yes," he stated. "I've never been more sure of it until now."

I hoped he was right.

"Why now?"

"Everything's lining up," he said. "You arrived, and our powers intensified. We went to the woods and actually saw him. And now Laney's freaking out. It's happening, Brynn. It's about to explode."

I lifted my hands to my face and pressed on the bridge of my nose.

"I know. I feel it, too," I agreed. "So, what do we do now?"

"We plan our return to the woods," he said. "I know what we need to look for."

I stared at him as my jaw dropped. He knew something and was going to share it.

"You do?" I asked.

He nodded. "In the woods, the day Tommy went missing, we were together. We were little, nine and ten years old, and easily intrigued by anything unusual." His sniggered, probably remembering their adventures. "We discovered an old wooden hut. It was the shape of a huge teepee, like, triangular. It was falling apart, and I remember seeing a dead bird by the entrance. It spooked us, but our curiosity led us further." He took a breath. "Tommy leaned into the doorway first and saw a strange glow inside, almost like the embers of a fire." He hesitated for a moment, then continued. "As he stepped in, he cried out to me as if he were lost. His voice trailed into oblivion as I stared into the emptiness of the hut."

"What the hell?" I gasped.

"A strange cackling surrounded me from the darkness of the trees. It sounded like an evil witch and scared the shit out of me." He glanced over. "I ran after that."

He drove in silence for a few moments, clearly suffering from the guilt of leaving his friend.

"All the parents and the police came back with me to search for him. It was hours later, though. Laney's mother had distracted them all, sending them to the wrong location at first. She insisted on having seen a hut before, too, but brought them to the wrong side of the woods. I could never understand why she did that."

My eyes widened just from hearing of her involvement.

"We searched all through the night. But no matter where we looked, I couldn't find the hut. No one believed me anymore. They just thought I was making it up to cover for having lost my friend." He swallowed hard as the final word squeaked out of him.

"That's horrible," I murmured, closing my eyes against the sadness.

We drove in silence for several minutes, then he spoke again.

"Minister and Ms. Kelly both believed me. No one else did," he said. "I've stayed in close touch with them all these years and let them know any time I sense Tommy's presence. You know, with my gift, I have the luxury of feeling other people's emotions. So, yeah, I feel his terror sometimes. I feel his desperation to be found. And then when I tell his parents, I feel their grief all over again, their sorrow. It's killing me."

I sucked in air after having stopped breathing for a minute.

"We're going to end this, Shane. For the Kelly's... and for you. I swear I'll do whatever it takes."

He gave a weak smile and then pulled over at the side of a bridge.

"Come on," he said, climbing out of the car. "I want to show you something."

∼

We scrambled down a steep embankment of crushed gravel and landed by the edge of a river. The water moved by at a fast rate, carrying a slick of foamy slime along with it.

"There's supposedly an old Indian burial ground around here somewhere." He glanced around. "I've looked for it a million times." He shrugged. "But this is what I want you to see." He led me toward the base of the bridge.

My eyes moved along the immense arch beneath the overpass and landed on the colorful graffiti on the far side.

He brought me to a landing at the base of the arch. We stood on the wooden boards, and I dizzied from the sight of the massive span of curved concrete that loomed above us.

"Wow. This is-*is-is*...," my voice echoed, and I stopped in surprise. Then I started again. "This is amazing-*ing-ing*...." My voice bounced through the archway in a perfect rhythm of echoes.

Shane turned to the arch and shouted, "Bah!"

His voice bounced a million times, fading into oblivion.

"That's crazy," I squealed.

"It's why they call it Echo Bridge," he said.

"I love it." I clapped to hear the sound reverberate into hollow nothingness, like a lost abyss.

Shane grew somber for a moment. "The sound reminds me of Tommy's screams when he disappeared."

My face dropped.

"Oh, shit," I whispered.

"No, it's okay," he assured me. "I come here to remember him. It's like hearing him again, in a way."

I shuddered from the thought and wrapped my arms around myself.

"Sorry," he said, pulling his sweatshirt over his head. "Here, take this."

He shook it at me as I stared at him.

His tee-shirt had lifted when he pulled off the hoodie, exposing his stomach, and I nearly lost my shit. He was ripped. Like, rock-solid. I'd had no idea. Or I guessed, I'd just never thought about it before.

But now, I was a mess.

Holy shit.

"Um, thanks." I reached for his hoodie and pulled it over my head.

His warmth lingered in the soft fabric, and the smell of him overwhelmed my senses. It was fantastic.

I wrapped my arms around myself again, not knowing what else to do, praying he wasn't picking up on my reaction to him.

But I knew he was.

A slight smirk teased at the sides of his mouth, and I just wanted to die.

I'd been so distracted by Dom's classic attractiveness, I hadn't noticed how hot Shane was. I'd never been the cougar-type, so just hadn't thought about him in that way.

Well, shit, he'd caused a complete one-eighty in me now, and in the present moment, I could no longer function.

"I didn't mean to make you nervous," he said. "Sorry, I can feel it." He shook his head like he was only making matters worse. "Ugh, this is so awkward. Like, we can't hide shit like normal people. It's annoying."

I chuckled.

He was trying to lighten the moment and was actually doing an okay job of it.

"It's okay," I said. "I'm just not used to people being nice to me. I react all wonky and shit."

He grinned. "You think I'm nice?" he teased.

My fist shot out and punched him in the arm before I could stop it. "No," I teased back. Then I turned back toward the massive arch and shouted, "What the fuck is going on-*on-on*...?"

The sound of my cry bounced back at us, over and over, making us laugh.

Shane called out, "This fucking sucks-*sucks-sucks*!" And the sound echoed into our bones.

"Shit! Fuck-*fuck-fuck*...!" I screamed, and his voice mixed with mine as he shouted the same.

We buckled over in laughter from our lewd display, but the catharsis was worth it.

"I feel better now," he said.

"Yeah," I agreed with a chuckle. "Me too."

## CHAPTER 20

For the rest of the week, we all strategized as discreetly as possible. Ms. Kelly hadn't returned, and we knew our focus had to be on getting her pardoned. From their perspective, she appeared to be a negligent educator placing her students at risk, but that was because she'd kept the academy a secret.

She had to.

We were different, and no one would be willing to believe what we were capable of. There was enough history of people being put away in mental hospitals for symptoms similar to ours.

Ms. Kelly would never expose us like that.

Instead, she helped us to embrace our gifts and strengthen them. Her mentoring was life-changing for all of us. We each believed we were weird or strange in some way like we didn't fit in. But it was because we were unique and powerful.

Sending us on these projects was her way of training us. Sure, it may have seemed irresponsible to the untrained eye, but we knew her methods were necessary, and we had the protection of our powers.

The only way to redeem her good name was to complete our project and show that her leadership created growth within each of us —more than any classroom could ever achieve.

Then I thought about the closed-minded school committee members and Principal Haney's tunnel vision. They'd never see Ms. Kelly for what she truly was. They only wanted bland educators who would follow the letter of the law to the T.

My wondering thoughts paused.

What *was* Ms. Kelly, anyway? I'd seen her true essence, and it was unworldly.

Honestly, I wasn't even sure what the options were for labeling her.

She understood each of us and our abilities more than we even did. Then she had the power to enter our thoughts at the most crucial moment. And there was probably more she was capable of.

I didn't know why I'd never thought about it before. I just assumed she was more in tune with supernatural occurrences and fostered it when she picked up on it in others.

Naive.

Ms. Kelly was more.

A lot more.

But something was holding her back. Something kept her confined within her own abilities.

And I was determined to find out what.

She needed to be freed. In every way.

And finding Tommy was the first step.

I hadn't seen Laney at all for a few days, until she flashed her smug grin at me in the hallway, reminding me of her incessant existence.

Seeing her reminded me that all I wanted to do was get out of the school. It was Friday afternoon, and we'd suffered long enough with our self-imposed separation and brutal confinement within stagnant classrooms.

The grin on Laney's face had caused my stomach to turn. It was like she thought she'd won something and flaunted her intangible victory around the school. But the arrogance in her gaze held more than that as if she knew something we didn't. It wove insecurity through my gut.

And annoyingly, her minions didn't hesitate for a second in their worship of her next-level status, regardless of the fact they had no clue what was really going on. They followed her like eager puppies, flipping their hair at me and giggling as they passed. The degrading power of their giggle was maddening.

Laney thought she'd silenced me. She believed Dom had moved on.

That was her internal victory.

But that was the furthest thing from the truth.

I hadn't been silenced.

If anything, I'd grown louder these past few days—my senses ready to explode.

And Dom hadn't moved on.

He'd actually focused his attention harder on me, and it burned my ass. It was as if he knew I'd been distracted by Shane recently, which pulled my attention away from him. So, he didn't hesitate to up his game.

Dom may have been silent these past few days, but his staring eyes gripped me, frequently. I caught his burning gaze every time I felt him enter my thoughts. It was like the heat of lasers burning into me, creating images of his animalistic hunger. The feeling raised my desire to levels of craving, and I fought against the urges that he awakened within me. The mixed signals between us messed with my head as I struggled to keep boundaries in place.

I shook the distracting thoughts away as I breezed past Laney's stare-down and moved toward the front entrance of the school to make my great escape. The weekend had finally arrived, and I was sure this would be a big one.

As I turned the final corner, the main office came into view, and I noticed a buzz outside the door.

Scanning the group of students that hovered by the windows, my eyes landed on Shane's. He held my gaze with focused concern. At that same moment, a sensation of alarm shot through me as his thoughts meshed with mine.

Something wasn't right.

As I held his gaze, attempting to understand what was happening, I bumped to the side after being knocked by someone. My attention broke away from Shane as I turned to whoever had just crashed into me.

Intense heat radiated off him as I gazed up and met Dom's wide eyes. Energy surged off him as if he were burning up from a fever, but instead of looking sickly, he was pumped up, ready to detonate.

He leaned into me and whispered near my ear, "This weekend."

The side of my face warmed from the heat of his breath, and I flinched from the shock of it.

Attempting to remain aloof in front of the other students, I nodded slightly while keeping my eyes averted.

He moved past me and shot out the doors with a loud smash.

My face reddened from the strange encounter, and I stared at the ground, recovering from the unusual sensations he'd awakened in me. How did he have the power to do that, every time? I squeezed my eyes shut to push away the lingering shivers.

Trying to refocus, I thought about his words. All he'd said was, "This weekend." Two words that screwed with my mind. Was it an innuendo? Or was he focused on finally getting to work on our project? As much as the butterflies in my stomach wanted the first tempting option, I had to stay focused on our mission and believe he was doing the same.

He was ready to go back.

Ready for all of us to go back.

And the intense energy surging off him proved he was ready for a fight.

I took a deep inhale and looked toward the office windows to see what all the excitement was about. In that same instant, my eyes met Shane's again.

His unblinking stare confirmed he'd watched every detail of my encounter with Dom. And probably picked up on my feelings around it as well.

I pulled my eyes away from his and cursed myself.

Fuck.

This was getting more complicated than we needed right now. Our focus had to remain steady on Ms. Kelly and our project. Any other distractions could derail our mission.

Feeling Shane's eyes still on me, I moved closer to the office windows and looked in.

Standing among the principal and the school resource officer was Laney's mom. Her perfectly coiffed blonde hair and high-end designer outfit emanated a sense of authority that the others responded to without question. As a member of the school committee, she held full command of whatever was discussed, as if she held supreme power within the group. The others listened and nodded, causing my stomach to turn.

I shot my eyes back to Shane's.

We pushed all other concerns aside and focused only on the current situation that unfolded in the office.

Our thoughts collided, erupting in panicked unison. "She's on to us. We don't have much time."

∼

I sailed out of the school to get as far away as possible from Mrs. Rosco and her posse. She had them all tightly wound around her finger, knowing she had their employment contracts under her thumb. Being a member of the school committee held considerable power over the school officials, and they knew it.

Shane pushed through the other students and followed me out of the school. I felt his angst tearing after me, so I sped up. The last thing we needed was to be seen interacting, but I could tell he was ready to throw that to the wind.

I rushed past the wrought iron entry gates of the school and shot around the corner. Right away, the chaos of the school quieted behind me, and I let out a huge exhale. It was crazy the level of intrigue that lady was able to conjure, and I was happy to leave it far behind me.

Before I could pull the next breath in, Shane rushed around the corner, nearly smacking right into me.

"Shit," he hissed, pulling back apologetically.

I turned to keep walking.

"We shouldn't be seen together," I warned. "It's too crazy right now."

"Wait," he said.

I glanced at him quickly and then pulled my eyes away.

He froze, not knowing what to say next, and hung on the suspended moment.

My first instinct was to save him from the awkward tension and his desperation to know what was going on. But I didn't have an answer. My mind spun with everything that was going on, and I couldn't think clearly.

In the silence between us, he pulled my arm to get me to look at him again. I fought to keep my eyes steady in the direction of home, but his plead over-powered my sensibility, and I turned to him.

He held my gaze with an intensity I hadn't felt before. It burned into my soul, igniting me from inside. He poured his heart into me— his insecurities, his desires, his pain, and his hopes. All of him.

I gasped at the rush to my senses, and my heart rate accelerated, pounding in my ears. Breathless, I stared into his eyes, wanting nothing more than to fall into his arms. The rush overwhelmed me as every nerve in my body responded to him.

He reached for my other arm and stepped closer. Our proximity sent heightened excitement through me, making me lose all sense of time and place.

I only saw *him*.

I only felt *him*.

His eyes moved to my mouth as he pulled in his bottom lip. Mesmerized, I stared as it glistened, and my muscles went limp.

In that instant, a horn blared as a car pulled up next to us.

"Get in!" Poorva shouted from the open window.

# CHAPTER 21

Poorva gunned it and pulled away from the school before Shane and I were fully settled. Her anxiety filled the car, leaving us more breathless than we already were.

"Dudes, this is insane," she blasted. "There's no way I'm jeopardizing my scholarship to Stanford."

Her comment sent my head spinning in a completely new direction.

"What?" I twisted my body to face her.

Shane moved to the middle of the back seat and leaned up between us. "Poorva?"

Her words caught us off guard. First of all, we'd been focused on something completely different that still fluttered in my stomach, but now it sounded like she was considering dropping out of the project. The tingles in my belly instantly turned to nausea.

Shane and I leaned in farther, questioning her loyalty to the project. We'd never heard this type of waver in her voice before.

"No," she said. "This one is getting out of hand. Ms. Kelly's been fired. Now the school committee and the police are involved. You guys don't understand. This could ruin everything for me."

I pressed my head into the back of my seat in shock. How could she pull out now? This was the moment we'd all been working toward. It was time to finish this.

I looked back at Shane, and he held the same panicked look in his eyes that I felt.

"Poorva, please," I said. "We need you. We have to stick together as a team to fix all of this. We're not as strong when we're broken apart."

She shook her head. "It's bigger than you guys realize."

It was like she knew something we didn't. Something had frightened her, and now she was ready to jump ship. But we couldn't afford to lose her. Ms. Kelly had formed our group, with everyone's gifts in mind, and we needed to stick together. Poorva's gifts were different from any of ours, and without her, we'd have an exposed vulnerability.

We had to convince her to stay.

"Did you see something?" Shane asked. "Something unusual?"

I twisted my head to him and stared. What could he be talking about? Did Poorva see things?

He looked at me, pressing his lips together in resignation. It was clear to me then that he knew what Poorva was capable of. Maybe even more than she did.

She slowed the vehicle, then pulled over to a stop. Cars whizzed by as the pressure within ours mounted. Shifting in her seat, she faced us both with a worried look that twisted my gut.

"I usually just see auras," she said. "You know, colors and energy around people."

"Chakras," I stated, encouraging her to keep going.

She nodded. "But, it's more now." She swallowed hard. "I see intentions behind the colors. I see glimpses of events."

Shane pressed closer. "Precognition."

Poorva glanced at him and murmured, "Yes."

Holy shit. Poorva's skills were developing quickly—faster than she could handle. It made sense that her first instinct was to run. But this was the moment of truth—when all of our gifts combined were making an exponential difference.

"Rule number one—don't run," I stated.

The car fell silent.

I waited a moment for my words to sink into her. She turned her eyes front, avoiding my pressure-filled gaze, but I knew she was fuming. Her loyalty went too deep, and no matter how frightened she was, she wouldn't be able to abandon us now.

My eyes widened with curiosity. "What are you seeing, Poorva? You have to tell us."

She twitched with anxiety and swallowed hard.

Holy shit. Whatever she had seen was causing some serious discomfort—enough to make her want to bail entirely.

No matter how uncomfortable it might be, we needed the information. This was exactly why we were the chosen ones for the project. Our gifts allowed for higher perception that gave us a great advantage. We needed whatever it was that Poorva had picked up on so we could prepare for what we were walking into.

I stared at her, waiting for an answer.

Shane repeated my question. "What did you see, Poorva?"

She fidgeted in her seat, and ran her fingers through her hair, pulling it away from her face. She glanced at each of us and then took a deep breath.

With a low whisper, she said, "We lose."

The blood drained from my head, and I felt dizzy. Poorva's premonition was the worst news we could ever hear.

We lose.

Her words were terrifying. Not only in what might happen to us in the woods, but also from the idea that we don't accomplish what we need to do. Her words meant we were unsuccessful in our project.

We couldn't save Tommy.

We couldn't save Ms. Kelly.

Our futures would all be compromised.

"We can't lose," I stated. "It's not an option."

Poorva stared at me with sunken shoulders.

"She's right," Shane said. "It's not an option. Tell us exactly what you saw, and we'll figure out a way to change it. Losing is not what we do. This project is everything we've trained for, Poorva. We got this."

She shook her head. "If I get kicked out of school, my life is over. Going to med school is everything *I've* trained for. This other stuff is not what I signed up to do."

My wind was knocked out of me. I had no idea Poorva struggled with her two colliding worlds. The UMAs and our project meant everything to me, so I just assumed it was the same for the others.

"Okay, so we get expelled. Is that what you saw?" Shane asked.

He pushed her to keep perspective.

"That's the least of it," she mumbled. "First, we get our asses kicked in the woods, like, some of us are changed forever. We either lose our minds, or they're stolen from us. Then we're accused of endangering others and delinquency." She exhaled. "No matter what, we're screwed."

I turned my gaze and stared out the window. It didn't sound that far-fetched. I wouldn't be surprised if some of us lost our minds in the process. The level of terror we were about to face was enough to make anyone lose touch with reality. And add the supernatural elements to the equation, and shit, it's a recipe for disaster.

But we knew all this going in. We had to keep focus and rely on our unique abilities.

"Mrs. Kelly's first rule," I repeated. "Don't run."

Poorva huffed. "No, this is where the other rules come into play, Brynn. Believe what you see. Follow your gut. Run!"

"No," Shane spat. "It's not time for those rules yet. Brynn's right. Rule number one, don't run."

I glanced at him and nodded in agreement.

Poorva threw her hands up in exasperation. "Whatever." She rolled her eyes. "We're fucked."

"Yeah, maybe," Shane said. "But we're fucked either way."

"How so?" Poorva barked.

"If we do nothing... if we walk away now, we have to live with knowing we didn't do anything. How's that going to feel every day?

Knowing we're special. Knowing we had the power to do something but didn't use it." He glared at her. "I don't know about you, but I couldn't live with myself if I turned a blind eye and walked away now."

Poorva grimaced and turned to the wheel. She pulled out into traffic and drove in silence.

My phone buzzed in my backpack, and I grabbed it.

Dom's name lit up.

*Whats the plan*

I turned to Shane and caught him staring at my phone. His lifted eyebrow exposed his snooping.

"Tell him we're meeting at the woods tomorrow. Seven o'clock."

Poorva kept her foot heavy on the gas and drove without a flinch.

∽

Okay.

So we were meeting at the woods tomorrow at seven o'clock. Having a concrete plan for the start of the final stage of the project kept my eyes wide and my mind racing.

The safety of my bedroom, as I counted the minutes to morning, didn't have its typical secure feeling. Poorva had dropped me off after we drove the afternoon away, while Shane and I talked her off the ledge, and now I was left to stew in my own thoughts.

Tomorrow would be the moment of truth—the time that we would face our fears and use our powers to break apart a curse that had plagued the town for years.

Holy shit.

I was scared.

And now with Poorva's wavering loyalty, I worried about our ability to even do this. I prayed she would come back to us. Fully.

I supposed I couldn't blame her, though. Our last visit to the woods had resulted in a near annihilation from the local witch, as well as a complete mindfuck that made us think Tommy was still alive. And here we were, planning our next visit to the lovely town woods.

My entire body trembled in spastic quakes, and I clung to my pillow for security.

I laid on my bed, glad that Poorva had dropped me off before anyone could change their minds about our plan.

Shane had seemed adamant about the meeting time, and Poorva didn't challenge it. She'd already made her reservations clear—her personal stakes, which included her entire future in the medical profession. If she lost her chances at Stanford, in her mind, she was finished.

But the stakes went even higher than that.

We each had our own cost in this project, some worse than others. Losing the trust of a parent, or losing social status in school were the surface issues. Losing one's mind to tortured pain that was only present in the psyche, that was a big one. But the worst in my mind was Shane's. He'd be losing the opportunity to save his friend. To rescue the Kelly's only son. His stakes were enormous.

But the more I thought about it, the price of our collective mission was beyond any measure. It was bigger than any of us could fathom.

Saving Tommy.

How could that even *be* measured? There was no argument that could stand up to what we knew we needed to do.

And finding the witch—exposing her, before anyone else could be harmed by her eternal curse—it left no room for argument. If we weren't able to end her evil presence, then we might as well hand-feed more children to her and accept the damnable fate of this town.

My hands clenched into fists as I resolved to end her.

To end the craziness that had lured me here.

*Lured me?*

It was true.

I'd known I was different my entire life. Something had been preparing me for this day, training me to be able to face this supernatural occurrence. Every experience of my life had strengthened me in some way for this. And I was ready.

Ready to face the challenge of my life.

With my friends by my side.

And with every ounce of my strange quirkiness that made me who I was.

But how?

I had never fit in anywhere before, so what was it that made me fit into *this*? There had to be a connection... to something.

And I was afraid I was about to find out.

## CHAPTER 22

Our cryptic text messaging made it clear when and how we should meet at the woods.

Communication had to remain at a minimum, particularly now that the police were involved. Who knew what they were able to track and trace. And not only that, but Laney and her mother had seemed to figure out too much about our group, and we had no idea where they got their information. So, we did our best to keep everything as secret as possible.

The time had finally come.

We were ready to carry out the final step of our project—the ultimate conclusion.

My muscles twitched with nervous excitement as I prepared for the showdown, and I struggled with even the most mundane tasks. Fumbling through my preparation, it felt like I blinked, and then it all began.

We rendezvoused at the school as planned, leaving our vehicles parked out of sight to avoid any suspicion of our gathering. That way, we wouldn't have to park at the trail opening of the woods, drawing unwanted attention to our mission.

"Let's break into our teams now," Shane said. "We'll be less conspicuous in smaller groups." He waved for Poorva and Blake to join him. "If any cars drive by, try to dip behind a bush before you're seen. We don't need any unwanted attention before we even get there."

We grabbed our gear, each with a small pack of supplies, and Dom and Courtney waited with me as Shane's team headed out first.

"Once we get to the woods, we can regroup with them," I confirmed to my team, as much for my own sake as theirs.

Courtney gave a quick nod.

Dom stared at me, breathing heavily as if he'd just run a 5K.

"Are you okay?" I watched him through narrowed eyes.

He was either experiencing the start of a panic attack or was about to throw up.

"Yeah, I'm good," he panted. "Let's go. I need to use some of my energy before I jump out of my skin." He shifted his weight back and forth.

Courtney glared at him as if he had no idea what it meant to endure discomfort. The steel-lock that clamped across her face showed the level of control she exerted over her own internal pain. Her restrained shaking caused Dom to hesitate, and he dropped his eyes to the ground.

"Sorry," he said. "I got this."

He balled his fists and paced back and forth like a caged animal.

I approached Courtney and reached for her. Just before touching her arm, I stopped, afraid to either hurt her or harm myself. I'd channeled her pain once before and never, ever, wanted to know that feeling of torturous burning again. I had no idea how she'd endured it for so long. It was no wonder she could hardly speak. Ever.

Several minutes later, I turned in the direction of the woods. "Okay. Let's go."

It didn't take long to walk beyond the residential area and enter the more remote section of the road. Five minutes into the walk, we were half-way there, and the sound of a car rumbled behind us. We hopped into the shelter of the trees and waited for it to pass. Music blasted out of the car, and a moment later, the smell of weed wafted past us.

"We're not the only ones headed to the woods tonight," Dom huffed. "They'll be gone by dark, I'm sure. No one has the balls to stick around here too late."

I hoped he was right. The last thing we needed was distraction or interference of any kind.

Up ahead, I saw the turn-in for the parking area for the trail. The others would be waiting for us there.

As we got closer, I noticed the car that had passed us earlier. It had pulled into a small alcove at the side of the road.

"Quiet," I whispered as we passed it.

The windows had already fogged up, and quiet giggles traveled out to us.

"Oh, how cute," Dom teased.

I exhaled in relief, knowing their intensions were unrelated to ours.

I kept my focus forward, heading straight for the lot.

As we turned into it, I glanced around, looking for our friends.

Nothing.

They weren't there.

"Where are they?" I said aloud. "They're supposed to wait for us right here."

A nervous twang twisted my gut. The plan was already falling apart.

Dom squared his shoulders. "They probably want to win," he said.

I shook my head. "No, they wouldn't do that." A twinge of suspicion ran through me, and I glared at Dom for even suggesting it. "Something must have happened." I looked around the area for any clues. "Maybe they went farther up the road."

"No, this is the only entry point on this side of the forest. They'd have to travel for miles to get to the next point." He glanced into the opening of the trail. "I think they went in without us."

I rubbed my eyes, straining to come up with a new plan.

Then, I saw something. Like the flash of a memory, only not from the past.

In my mind's eyes, I saw them running frantically, yelling and screaming. They were in trouble, and their powers were tangled, leaving them defenseless.

"They're in there," I cried out. "I can see them."

Something was blocking their skills making it impossible for them to work together. Instead, they were struggling to hold onto their own sanity, fighting an unseen, insidious villain.

I gasped in horror. "Something's wrong. They need our help!"

Dom reached for me. "Wait." He held me back for a moment, tipping his head toward the trail opening.

He lifted his face into the air and breathed in deeply. "You're right. They were here," he said. "I smell them."

He twitched and tilted his head.

"I hear them, too," he said. "Their voices fill the space in the meadow."

I listened and heard nothing.

"Are you sure?" I begged.

His head tipped again as he listened harder. "Yes. Positive. There's an open gate to the spirit world. I smell it. And I hear it." He shook his head in an attempt to make it stop. His face crunched in a tight grimace as he fought his next words. "They're screaming Tommy's name."

With that, we tore down the trail into the darkness of the woods. The gray blanket of dusk turned to immediate black as the thick trees blocked the light of the rising moon.

Before long, we reached the gate that blocked the trail. Using the light from my phone, I scrambled over the rails while Courtney and Dom climbed over at the same time. The rattling of the metal gate made my hair stand on end, scared to death that we'd be heard.

Once over it, we hurried along the trail toward the clearing. Noticing the underbrush becoming sparser, it was clear we were getting closer. Once all overgrowth between the high trees was gone, leaving only dirt forest floor among the thick trunks, I knew we were almost there.

It was like a bomb had gone off at some point in the past, leveling all living things, leaving only the strongest trees in its wake. Then I realized, the clearing was likely the point of detonation.

Something big had occurred there once, leveling everything around it to dust.

And we were headed straight for it.

We continued to move at a quick pace until the opening at the end of the trail came into view. Dom's breathing was all I could hear, and the extreme heat radiating off him made sweat bead on my brow.

Whimpers escaped Courtney's throat as she quaked with spasms of rising pain.

My panic rose as I watched my friends reacting in heightened discomfort to the proximity to our target.

As we burst into the opening of the meadow, my inward sight opened up to visions of Shane, Poorva, and Blake, trapped and struggling to escape from a terrifying void.

I searched across the vast clearing for any sign of them. They were nowhere to be seen. Vanished without a trace.

Then a strange ripple vibrated near the far side of the open meadow. It was like a subtle wobble that shook the dark colors around it.

"Did you see that?" I pointed.

Courtney and Dom followed my gaze. Then the shimmer happened again.

"What the fuck is that?" Dom said.

He'd seen it too, and relief whooshed out of me.

"Come on!" I tore across the clearing, tripping on the uneven terrain. "It's got to be them!"

By the time we reached the far side, the rippling glow had dissipated. I searched frantically, reaching my hands all around in front of me in hopes of feeling something.

Dom and Courtney moved up behind me, searching into the darkness for any sign of it too.

With a gasp, Courtney pointed to the edge of the trees. Her hand trembled in quaking spasms.

"What the fuck is that?" Dom groaned again.

I stared into the trees, and my eyes focused on a tall wooden structure. Its triangular shape rose sharply toward the height of the trees, and at its base was a dark opening.

My breath stopped short as I recognized the strange dwelling. It was exactly as Shane had described it to me. He'd seen this structure before, when he was a kid... with Tommy.

But I was sure it wasn't here last time. We would have noticed its shadow looming at the edge of the clearing.

Then a flash of memory widened my eyes. When we saw Tommy on the trail the last time we were here, I had seen a similar structure hidden in the trees behind him. I gasped from the flood of the memory and knew it had to be the same hut.

I stared at its ominous presence, terrified to move any closer. Its rotted wooden planks fell away from the sides in jagged disrepair, but it still stood firm. A strange fog billowed at the base and swirled away from the dark opening as if encouraging us to enter.

"It's a trap," I whispered. "Luring us in." My air whooshed out of me, leaving me breathless. Terror rose in my throat as my next words struggled to come out. "They're in there."

As soon as the words left my mouth, we heard it.

Their cries for help.

Their voices echoed from deep within the darkness, as if trapped in a vast abyss. Sounds of pain and terror mixed in a torturous assault on our senses. I covered my ears and squeezed my eyes shut as Dom and Courtney did the same.

But it wouldn't stop.

"Let's go," Dom shouted, ready to run straight into it. "We need to get to them."

Just as we prepared to enter the ominous opening, their voices gained strength and commanded us. "Stay out!"

We reeled back in terror and stared into the darkness of the hut.

Then their voices churned again and blasted, "You'll be trapped forever!"

~

We lurched back, for fear of being sucked into the haunting structure.

"There has to be another way to get them out," I cried, looking around for anything that could help.

Courtney stepped back into the open space of the clearing.

"We need to lure her out," she said.

My head jerked to her. "What? Who?"

"The Dark Witch," she stated with confidence.

Her gaze went blank as she shifted in her new decision.

Dom moved closer to her.

"Courtney?" His voice trailed out of him. "What are you going to do?"

His tone proved he knew she was about to do something radical. Something unplanned.

"Courtney?" I pressed, following the two of them.

She moved closer to the middle of the open space and stood on the same spot she'd collapsed on last time.

"I don't care anymore," she cried out. "I'm not afraid of her. I just want it to stop."

She dropped her head back and lifted her arms out to the sides.

"Wait, Courtney," I screamed. "Stop!"

Her head tipped in my direction. "It's okay, Brynn. This is what was meant to be."

And in that instant, she burst into flames.

The blast of heat shot Dom and me back, leaving us panting. We stared at Courtney as fire engulfed her, lapping in every direction off her arms and hair.

As we stared in disbelief, a scream came from the direction of the trail.

"No!" the voice cried. "Stop!"

Racing from the woods, two figures barreled into the clearing.

Within seconds, they were upon us, and one of them went straight for Courtney. She reached right into the flames and shoved her. Courtney tumbled back but steadied herself again, resuming her sacrificial position within the fire.

The woman shoved at her again, this time reeling back from the intensity of the heat.

Frustrated, the two of them shot their razor-sharp attention to us.

As they moved closer, Dom and I cried out the same name.

"Laney?"

She bombed toward us with her mother on her heels.

"Make her stop!" she screamed. "She's killing her!"

I froze, staring into Laney's face.

The shock of seeing her there had blown my mind to bits. But then the fact that she made demands like she knew what was going on, that blew the rest of the pieces into oblivion.

Before I could ask questions, Laney's mom let out a blood-curdling cry of pain and dropped to her knees.

"Stop her," Laney screamed, turning to Courtney. "Please! She's hurting my mother."

With my eyes nearly bulging out of my head, I stared at Dom in panic. "What do we do?" I pleaded.

His breathing had hit an unnatural level, and he gave no response to anything around him. It was as if he was struggling to hold himself together and could focus only on that.

"Laney, tell me what's going on," I screamed. "It's the only way I can help."

She stared at her crouched mother in terror and then back to me.

"You have to stop her!" She pointed to Courtney. "That bitch is going to kill my mother!"

Courtney was in a trance of some form. The fire burned all over her, but she remained unharmed within it. The tranquil look on her face made her appear to be at peace. It was the first time I'd ever seen her that way, and relief washed through me.

"What are you talking about?" I shouted at Laney. "What does any of this have to do with you or your mother?"

Mrs. Rosco cried out in pain, and winced as the skin on her face blackened and peeled.

"Hurry!" Laney blasted.

I turned back to the wooden structure as the rotting boards began shuddering. The energy all around me grew to an atomic level, and my senses piqued to their highest point.

Laney's face flashed in my mind, then contorted into her mother's image. I studied the picture in my head and watched it morph into the haunting, twisted face of the Dark Witch.

They were all connected.

Somehow, through the history of this place, Laney's family was rooted in the evil of the Dark Witch.

I shot my eyes back to her and stared into her desperate face. In an instant, she recoiled, knowing I saw straight into the darkness of her soul.

"No," I shouted. "*You* have to stop her!"

# CHAPTER 23

Laney pulled back from my demand. I'd challenged her to stop the Dark Witch, and she cowered from my pressure.

"No, I can't," she cried. "This is how it's meant to be. It's the only way she can continue to live."

I stared at Laney in bewilderment. Somehow, she'd been allowing this curse to continue. She was actually protecting the Dark Witch.

"What the fuck are you talking about," I screamed at her. "Are you crazy?"

"Fuck you, Douglas," she seethed. "You can't just walk into this town and fuck it all up."

Her words punched me in the face, and I shook off the assault. She was clearly insane.

"You're seriously trying to defend what's going on here?" I hissed. "A boy is missing, you psycho bitch. Do you have any idea the pain that has caused?" I panted as anger surged through me. "And my friends are caught now. It's over, Laney. I'm ending this now."

I turned to the shanty structure that somehow held my friends within its unknown realm. The moment I moved toward it, a sickening scream gurgled out of Laney's throat as she launched for me. In the same instance, a burst of energy came from the wooden structure, followed by a terrifying cackling.

The Dark Witch was among us.

Her presence poisoned my veins as her evil permeated everything around me.

Courtney's arms began to shake, and her head rocked as her flames grew higher.

My eyes darted back to the hut and locked on a sinister figure moving out of its opening.

Covered in a black cloak, a hunched being glided toward us. Her bony frame created sharp angles beneath her coverings, and I stared at the shriveled hand that reached out toward us, pointing directly at me.

As the witch got closer, my heart stopped in pure terror. The glow of the flames behind me illuminated her face for a brief moment, exposing the blackened, charred skin.

My terror rose higher from the sight of her, sending me running for my life. As I turned away from her, I ran straight into Dom... and then passed through him. As I moved through his body, I felt all the power of his angst and the mounting pressure he held within his core. He was about to explode.

As I left his form and hovered just beyond him, I stopped short, panting.

*What the fuck?*

I looked back at Laney and the witch as they continued to move closer to me, but it was just my body they were approaching. My spirit was out here, moving freely.

Astral projection.

Ms. Kelly had taught us about it. The UMAs had been practicing, but no one had achieved it yet.

Until now.

I thought about what had just occurred. I had been so terrified by the image of the witch, I literally jumped out of my skin. It was more than that, though. It was a process that started in my mind, releasing me from the confines of my body, allowing me to explore without limits.

I could do it again. I was sure.

I ran back, past Dom, and jumped back into my body. The reconnection sent shivers through my every nerve, awakening me to a higher level of consciousness. Pushing my fear aside, I faced Laney and the ominous presence of the evil witch.

"Release them!" I commanded. I gestured toward the hut and then to Courtney. "Free them now!"

"Are you insane?" Laney laughed, unaware of what I had just experienced. "It would be suicide." She glanced at her mother's form crouched on the ground, rocking. "It's hereditary. Don't you see? We're of a bloodline that can't be stopped." She glanced at the Dark Witch and then into the blackness of her lair. Her gaze turned back to me then. "It's you that must be stopped."

With those words, the Dark Witch lifted her hand and moved it in circles across the front of me. I stepped back, and Laney lurched forward to grab me. Just as her arms went around me, I heard Dom's voice.

"Don't touch her, Laney," he shouted. His booming voice was more of a growl that echoed through the clearing.

"Fuck you, Dom. You simpleton. So easily seduced. It's pathetic," she spat. "We're taking her, just like the others, and you're well aware of what will happen to you if you disobey us."

Her arms squeezed around me tighter.

She didn't realize I was about to launch out of my body again, and head straight into the hut for my friends. In my astral form, I could help them without the danger of being trapped inside. Nothing could contain me while I was outside of my body.

My eyes closed, and before I could channel the leap, a roar shocked my eyes open.

I twisted toward the sound, and right before me, Dom leapt at Laney. In mid-flight, he exploded into a blur of gnashing teeth and black fur. The frenzied sound of a nuclear explosion landed right in front of me on four paws. It frothed at the mouth, sending hot breath into my face as it stared into my eyes.

My air rushed out of me in astonishment. I couldn't believe what I saw, but my heart told me that it was real.

It was him.

He'd shifted right before me, into a creature that could tear us all apart.

"Dom?" I whispered. "Oh my god."

His deep blue eyes stared into mine as steam shot from his flaring nostrils. A low rumbling growl vibrated from his strong neck, sending shivers through me.

Then the enormous head of the wolf turned to Laney and the others. The Dark Witch stepped back slowly as if threatened, and Laney stared in utter shock.

Her mother lifted her head, exposing the charred flesh on her face and screamed, "Run!"

∼

In the blink of an eye, Dom was on Laney.

She fell to the ground under the weight of the pouncing wolf, becoming pinned under his massive paws. His teeth snapped inches from her neck, causing her to scream.

"Help me!" she cried.

As Laney struggled beneath the wolf, the Dark Witch crept into the shadows and slipped out of sight. I saw the flap of her cloak trail behind her as she disappeared into her hut.

Laney's mother called out, "Stop the beast! He'll kill her."

I stared at Mrs. Rosco in disbelief. First, she was commanding her daughter to end me. Now, she was begging me to save her.

Either way, without hesitation, I jumped at Dom. I'd never known wolves could be so large, and the sheer size of him scared me to death. One wrong snap and he'd have my head. I prayed the creature could be reasoned with.

I approached him from the side and pushed my hand through the fur on his shoulder. It was thick and soft, and I felt the strong muscle ripple as I touched it. The wolf turned its head from Laney and looked at me.

"Dom, don't hurt her," I whispered into his twitching ear. "We need her help. Keep her pinned while I try to save the others."

He snorted with a huff.

"I need you to protect my body while I go in there," I added. "I'm going to leave it behind. Keep watch over it."

His head shook as he made a sneezing sound.

"Promise me."

A groan came from deep in his chest, and I knew he understood.

"Get him off me," Laney pleaded. "You can't do this."

"Shut up, Laney," I shot. "I don't know what twisted rituals you're into, but this is criminal. It's black magic."

She whimpered. "Well, you would too, if it was *your* family!"

"Like hell."

"If they burned your great-grandmother at the stake, you'd have a different story," she spat.

I froze in my tracks and redirected my attention back to her. "What did you say?"

Tears rolled from her eyes and trailed into her hair. "You think it's a burned down orphanage," she laughed. "Look around. Can't you see? It's a fucking arena. It's where they burned the witches while the entire town watched and jeered."

My eyes widened, and I stared over at Courtney. She continued to remain in her trance, flaming, and now it was clear. She was the symbol of the burning witches, taking on the physical torment of their suffering in her daily existence. Somehow, she'd been targeted as the physical manifestation of the torture. Without her, the twisted story of this place would all be lost and forgotten.

"It's a horrible thing that happened in history, Laney. But why keep it going?" I shouted.

She took a deep breath. "Because it's *my* history. *My* family. The soul of my ancestor is trapped here. She never crossed over because her death was violent and unjust."

My eyes widened.

That was it.

The Dark Witch was trapped in limbo because of her untimely, gruesome death. I gasped, picturing her methods at staying alive in her lonely, endless realm.

"And so to remain in existence, she kidnaps children? Stealing their souls?" My harsh tone left no question of my judgment.

"It's the only thing that keeps her alive." She pulled back from the wolf's intense glare. "And we won't let her die. If she dies, we lose *our* power, too."

And there it was.

The powers of the Dark Witch were passed on through the bloodline, but if she no longer existed, it would extinguish their magic too. They were fighting to keep hold of it and would stop at nothing to keep their family intact.

I thought about Laney's efforts at trying to stop me any chance she had, from the moment she met me. She wanted me gone from the school, gone from the town. She knew I held the power to stop her family's curse, even before I did.

No wonder she was such a bully. She hated this town for what it had done to her ancestry hundreds of years earlier. Her best payback was to be queen bitch to everyone in it and perpetuate pain and suffering at all cost.

And there was more than that. There was a specific connection to Tommy. It was becoming clear to me now.

Shane had told me of Laney's trickery around the time Tommy went missing. She was a part of it then, as well. And Mrs. Rosco, too. The two of them had a hand in his disappearance.

I stared at Laney in horror as the realization of the truth flooded me—the truth of what she had done.

"*You* lured Tommy here," I blasted. "Oh my god." My hand smacked over my mouth as tears filled my eyes.

My body trembled as it all came together.

"You stole him from his family to save your own. And you tried to get Shane, too," I choked. "And probably others." I hesitated and swallowed hard. "You knew we were coming here today, and now you've trapped my friends."

A wicked giggle escaped her lips as her mother crawled closer.

"You're a sick, twisted girl," I spat. "And I'm going to stop you."

Her mother dragged herself nearer to us.

"We'll get them all, Laney," her mother choked. "Don't you worry, love."

"Go on," Laney shouted at me. "Try to save them," she laughed. "You don't have it in you, bitch!"

Dom pressed his weight harder on her shoulders and growled in her face. Her mother backed off to lessen the threat.

"You don't scare me, dog," Laney hissed at the massive wolf. "You know I can destroy you with one word."

I stared at the wolf as he shrank from her threatening words. It made no sense that Laney could have that much power over him, and it sent deep anger through me.

His strength should be enough to conquer her, but it seemed like he had no clue about what he was actually capable of. I prayed that he would figure it out fast.

Dom was a goddamn werewolf.

*What the actual fuck?*

That was my friend right there, all furry and snarling and enormous. How was I so accepting of this insane situation?

The truth was, I'd always known it. I mean, not that he was a wolf, though now that I thought about it more, he kind of was—but the fact that his gift had the power to change his shape was insane.

Then I thought of my own new skill—the one where I could launch out of my body, and for the first time, I understood the enormity of our powers. Being sensitives was only the tip of the iceberg. We were full-blown supernaturals plunked right in the middle of a metaphysical war, and now our abilities were being tested big time.

Having no clue of what Laney held over Dom, I still knew it was strong—strong enough to hold him off, even in wolf form. But I couldn't waste any more time. I had to get my friends.

"Don't let her scare you, Dom," I shouted. "Don't give her that power. There's nothing she could say that could destroy you."

Laney laughed out loud. "Oh, such a supportive friend," she teased. "He won't be so cute once you know the truth."

"Shut up," I shouted at her.

The wolf lowered his head, hovering it right over her face, and let out a deep, rumbling growl. His power grew over her as he deflected her threats.

She started to speak again, and just as her words formed in my ears, I used my emotional energy and launched myself right out of my body.

With a whoosh of light and sound, I plunged out of my restricting muscles and bones, and floated. Looking down over Dom and Laney, I shuddered at the sight of them—a huge snarling wolf pinning a nasty girl who looked more dangerous than the ferocious creature. Her mother was held off to the side, afraid to get any closer to the two, and Courtney's flaming silhouette continued to fill the center of the clearing.

It was enough to make me want to fly far away and never return to such insanity, but just as I nearly lost my mind to the overload of what was happening, a voice filled my thoughts.

"Amazing, Brynn," she said. "Your power is growing faster than I realized it ever could. You've achieved astral projection." The pride in her tone made me smile.

"Ms. Kelly?" My inner voice called to her.

"I'm with you, Brynn. And I'm sure of it now," she said. "You are the one we've been waiting for. I remember the day you first got your powers, long ago. It was the same day Tommy went missing."

"What? How do you know that?" I asked.

"The moment he was taken, his energy whisked away in search of a worldly body." She paused. "It found you, Brynn. I knew the moment it did. I knew you existed and I prayed that one day you would find your way back home."

Holy shit. I had no idea what was happening to me. All I knew was that it felt like I was getting closer to finding Tommy.

"I'm going to find him, Ms. Kelly," I said. "No matter what happens. I'll bring him home to you."

*No matter what happened.*

I knew there was great risk involved.

If I found Tommy, I would pass his life force back to him to save him. Then what would happen to me?

I would sacrifice myself for him. There was no question I would do it.

And if I survived the transfer, I would have to accept living as a normal person without my gifts. That was the part that scared me the most.

How could I ever be content with normal again?

I realized there was no way to survive this fully.

And with that knowledge, I turned toward the witch's shed and then spoke to Ms. Kelly again.

"Be here when I come out," I said. "I won't come out without your son."

## CHAPTER 24

Ms. Kelly's voice faded from my mind as I moved closer to the high triangular shadow of the dilapidated wooden hut. She'd called to me as I got closer to the witch's lair, telling me her powers couldn't cross past the boundaries to the other realm. Before I could understand all of what she was saying, her voice drifted away entirely.

I immediately missed the comfort of having her in my head and wished she could have stayed with me. Having no clue how she found my thoughts, I wondered how close she had to be to get inside my mind. The rest of us hadn't had time to test the boundaries of our collective consciousness.

Finding Shane, Poorva, Blake, and Tommy was now my only focus.

Once I found my friends, I'd have to figure out how to free them from the strange abyss. Together, we could face the twisted family of witches.

Laney and her mother scared the shit out of me, but facing them seemed like something that was on our level. It was the Dark Witch that was next level. Terror deep within my bones was an understatement of how she made me feel. And there was so much unknown about her and her power. I hoped never to have to see her again.

But I realized that was an impossible wish. I'd have to face her if I was going to save my friends.

I reached the entrance to the shaking wooden structure and glanced back into the clearing. My physical body remained in the field as if I were still engaged in the stand-off. With that distraction in place, I turned back to the dark opening of the triangular form.

Cracks between the wooden planks allowed shards of moonlight in, enough to let me see that the interior was empty. My heart sank in disappointment as I struggled to figure out what to do next. By instinct, I trailed inside for a better look, and as soon as I passed through the doorway, a rush of hurricane-force wind pushed against me.

I glided through the storm of streaking black and gray gusts, undaunted by its extreme force. The torrents whipped past me as I traveled through a wormhole of some kind. As the tempest died down, my astral body sank to the ground, feeling the full weight of gravity return as if my physical body had rejoined me.

Whatever had happened through the storm, it was as if it sent me through a portal where I was my full self again. I blinked as my eyes adjusted to the darkness, and then mysterious, twisted trees filled my vision, surrounding me.

Items hung from the gnarled branches by strings, and I moved closer for a better look. An old yo-yo swung from a high branch, twirling on itself, and a few branches farther was a small shoe hanging from its shredded laces.

The snap of a twig made me jump, and I scanned the area behind me with twitching eyes. My breath quickened as a rustling sound grew nearer.

As I squinted into the darkness of the tangled branches, my gaze landed on a pair of red glowing eyes. A low, rumbling growl shot terror through me. Then more movement. More eyes. And a chorus of rumbling growls.

I was surrounded by hounds of hell, and by the sound of their hungry snarls, they were programmed to kill.

I turned and sprinted past the spindly trees, getting caught in their ragged branches as I flew through them. The curled branches grew thicker and wove into each other, making it nearly impossible to break through. I tore into the maze of intertwined twigs, enduring deep scratched to my face and hands.

The snarling of the hounds grew louder as they closed in behind me.

Panting in terrified gulps, I pulled myself past a thick trunk and ran face-first into a small wool coat, hanging on a branch from its hood. The brown jacket had cub scout patches sewn on it and would have fit a little boy. I pushed the coat away from my eyes, ready to let out a horrified scream when my focus landed on an old, ramshackle house with boarded-up windows.

Looking back to see if the hounds were on top of me yet, glaring red eyes pierced my vision, and I ran for my life toward the derelict ruin.

The two-story, high gabled house loomed over me as if waiting for me to enter. Its blackened, boarded-up windows watched me as I barreled toward it. Jumping up the stairs at the small porch entrance, I grabbed onto the tarnished brass doorknob, frantically twisting it.

The dark clapboard exterior splintered, and shingles of rotted wood hung loosely, ready to fall apart at the slightest gust of wind. The condemned house seemed ready for demolition, though it could easily have been deemed a historical site from the 1600s... if anyone actually knew it was even there. Or cared.

Just as the door released from its housing, I fell inside and slammed it shut behind me before the hounds could get their claws and teeth in me. The snapping jaws and low growls died off as they retreated into the shelter of the mangled trees.

Panting, I scrambled to my feet and squinted into the darkness, searching for any sign of inhabitants. I moved across the empty room to the far wall where strange markings caught my attention. As I focused on the carvings next to a large fireplace, my ears twitched, remaining alert for any sound around me.

I reached my hand to the markings on the wall and trailed my fingers over them. With a gasp, I stepped back as the shape of a bunny with long ears and a bushy tail took form. My heart rate shot to the roof as I stared at the shape created from scratches in the damp wall. The scratch marks trailed off to the sides in streaks of five lines, like fingernails that clawed desperately into the surface.

"Tommy?" I called out by instinct, then fell silent again, listening.

A creaking sound of shifting boards pulled my attention to the corner of the room, and I darted toward it. In the shadows was a narrow passage of stairs leading up. Lowering my head to enter the small stairwell, I climbed the uneven, rickety steps that led to the second floor.

Slanted ceilings created a high-peaked loft area, and streaks of moonlight illuminated the musty space through gaps in a small boarded window at the front.

Like the downstairs room, this one was empty as well, and I stepped to the single window to try to see out. As I got closer to it, my eyes focused on streak marks across the thick, fogged glass. Stick figures came clear, and I stared at the shapes of small people running and falling away from a larger, dark figure in the middle.

I stepped back from the window, gasping for air as my eyes darted all around the room. In an instant, more claw marks in the walls became apparent, and as terror mounted, my eyes landed on broken letters toward the bottom.

The carved lettering pulled together as I got closer and read, "H E L P M E."

My heart pounded in my ears as I read the message scratched into the rotting wood of the wall. Someone had been trapped in here, frightened, calling for help. My eyes bulged from my head as I stepped back from the haunting words.

Just as I turned back for the stairs, I heard it.

Like an echo at first, the sound of voices seeped up through the floorboards. It sounded like it was coming from outside, but as I leaned into the stairwell to hear better, it was clear the voices were traveling from somewhere within the house.

"Shane?" I screamed. "Poorva?" My voice scratched out of me in terror.

I barreled down the narrow stairs and tripped on a loose board. My foot caught in the jagged wood of the broken step, and I fell into the sidewall, bumping my head. Dizzy and disoriented, I stumbled down the rest of the stairs and fell onto my knees with a crash.

With a loud gasp, I froze in place and held my breath, listening.

At first, only silence filled the empty room, but then as if from a far off place, the sound of their voices cried out to me again.

"Brynn...."

The sound of my name shot my eyes wide, and my breath burst in and out of me. Tears of terror pooled in my lower lids, and I squinted to clear them away.

"I'm here!" I shouted, desperate to find my full voice. "Where are you?" I called to them.

As I strained to listen harder, movement from the far corner of the room caught my eye. From the darkness, a figure moved out of the shadows and glided closer to me.

My heart stopped as I stared at the shrouded silhouette with a large hood over its head.

My shaking hands rattled in front of me as I covered my face, pushing the blur of wetness from my eyes to see more clearly. Blinking through the dusty streams of moonlight, I focused on her as she moved closer to me.

The Dark Witch.

As if frozen in place, my muscles refused to follow my command to run. Instead, I remained motionless in terror, waiting to see what she would do.

As I fought my defiant muscles, straining to run for my life, her voice filled my head with its sinister, gravelly sound.

"They've been waiting for you," she hissed.

Her voice filled my head as if it hadn't actually left her mouth. My heart seemed to stop as I realized we were connected telepathically.

Pulling in a huge breath of air, I gathered my wits, knowing I had to face her now, even though my body resisted.

"I'm here to take them home," I said in my mind, staring straight at her cloaked form.

"Mmm," she hummed. "How sweet of you."

She moved closer, and I balled my fists by instinct.

"It's over," I stated. "You've held on long enough. It's time for you to accept your fate and cross over."

She stopped short for a moment, then leaned in, as if examining me.

"You have no idea what you're talking about," she cackled. "Just like all the others. The leaders of this town may have passed through several generations, but they're all still the same. Controlling. Judging. Executing." Her voice hit a shrill snarl. "They must be punished."

Her last words stiffened my spine, but I pushed through my fear.

"What happened to you was a horrible, shameful crime. But these people you're hurting now, they're innocent."

"No!" she blasted. "There is no innocence here." Her shadowy form moved closer to the point where she hovered over me. "The minister. The lawyer. The town administrators. They are all to blame."

I thought of Ms. Kelly's husband, Michael. Then Poorva's father—the town attorney. And then Blake and Shane, their parents were involved in the town council, as well as other political involvement.

The Dark Witch was right.

The generations had evolved, but the leadership roles in the town were the same. And the Dark Witch held blame over them, just as Laney and her mother did.

"But these aren't the people who hurt you," I insisted.

"Oh, but they are. You see, the sins of our ancestors never die," she moaned. "My minister blamed me for using black magic. The town lawyer found me guilty. Then the administrators abused the power of their positions against me. They are the guilty ones." Her voice grew louder and more deranged. "And they will suffer."

I shrank back from her hovering form.

Her words cut into my soul as I felt the depth of her pain and her need for revenge. She targeted the loved ones of those whom she believed were responsible for her violent execution.

Caught in a state of limbo now, she required life force to remain in existence. How else would she be able to carry out her vengeance? Once that life force was snuffed, she would no longer exist. And she knew it.

She reached out to me as if craving to touch my energy. Her charred, bony hand became exposed as the cloak fell away from it. I pulled back from the unnerving sight and hissed in fear.

"Frightening?" she hacked. "Yes. What they did to me was barbaric." She pulled her hand back into her coverings. "But what they did to my sister was far worse."

*Sister? Jesus.*

Their line of witches went further than I realized. I wondered if we'd ever be able to stop them.

She continued. "They forced my beloved sister into a stout barrel through which long spikes had been driven. They rolled her down a hill and burned her mangled remains at the site where she landed. All for bewitching the men of the town with her beauty and charm. Her lovely nature brought on her demise."

She hesitated as if remembering her sister.

Then she added, "When I exposed the leaders for their weakness in the loins, they accused me of similar witchcraft. Their heinous accusations awakened my dormant powers.

Unknowingly, they had unlocked my dark magic, and as I burned in the public execution, I vowed to forever make them suffer."

# CHAPTER 25

The Dark Witch's thoughts filled my mind as I scrambled to keep up with her story. I couldn't be sure if she realized the extent to which I could read her thoughts, but either way, it was clear that the pain she had endured was excruciating, even now.

As much as I could empathize with the torture she had experienced, it still didn't justify her actions now. She had to release her pain and her hate, and cross over. But it was clear she had no intention of doing so.

She had made a vow.

Her vengeance was strong, and her only focus was prolonging the pain and suffering for those who betrayed her.

If I could convince her of my empathy, maybe I'd have a chance at rescuing my friends and getting out of there.

"Do you realize your family is out there now, suffering?" I spoke gently.

The witch stood taller, at attention. "No. They are powerful. My magic connects to them without yield."

"Yes, they share some of your power. But Laney, she's weakening. People are noticing her connection to the darkness. She'll be exposed for Tommy's disappearance. Her mother will also take blame."

It was true. The town was about to learn who was truly responsible for the curse on Lakefield and its innocent inhabitants. The Dark Witch's bloodline would be exposed.

"No, their powers are too strong. They'll avoid persecution." Her words held steady, but she still shrank from my premonition.

"They'll face the barrel and the stake of our modern society," I stated, knowing the threat would strike her deepest vulnerability.

The Dark Witch hunched over as if being hit in the gut. A deep wail churned from her throat as she cried out in pain. Her arms lifted around her as she invited the suffering to encompass her.

As she swayed in despair, I turned in the direction I'd heard my friends calling from... and bolted.

Behind the stairwell, I found a small door hidden in the shadows. I pulled it open, and in an instant, their voices wrapped around me, pulling me into the darkness.

I stumbled down uneven stone stairs and trailed my hands along the rocky sidewall for stability. The stale air held a chill as the temperature plummeted in the depths of the cold, damp cellar.

I kept my eyes wide open to see in the pitch blackness, but it was impossible. The complete absence of light created a thick blanket of nothingness.

"Shane?" I whispered. "Are you here?" My hands felt the space in front of me as I moved farther in.

As I held my breath, waiting for a hopeful response, a glow pulled my attention to the far corner of the basement.

I stared at a single point of yellow illumination, and then another. Then another.

My jaw dropped open as I gazed into the glow of my friend's energy fields. They stood together in a circle and reached out to me.

"Brynn!" Poorva cried. "I can't believe you found us."

Poorva had transferred her ability of seeing chakras to all of us, and the glow allowed us all to see each other in the darkness.

Shane cupped his hand over his mouth in disbelief.

Tears fell from my eyes as I hurried over to them. Shane pulled me into his arms as Poorva and Blake reached around me as well. We embraced each other with shaking sobs.

After a moment, they released their hold of me and stepped back slightly. They moved aside, exposing a small form hiding behind them.

My air whooshed out of me at the sight of him.

"Tommy?" I whispered.

His little face turned up at me, and he cowered behind Shane.

"It's okay, Tommy," Shane said. "She's our friend. She's here to help us."

I smiled and lowered myself to his level. Reaching my hand out, I said, "Nice to meet you, Tommy. I've heard so much about you." He took my hand and squeezed it. "Oh, you're strong, that's..."

My voice caught in my throat as his energy passed through me. Instead of taking his life force back from me, he sent more of it into me. His gift was alive and powerful.

I looked at the others, and they nodded.

"Sure, he's Ms. Kelly's boy. Of course he's got the touch," Shane said. "Just too young to know how to use it yet."

"It's why she wants him," Poorva said, glancing up the stone stairs to the space the witch inhabited.

"She plans to kill us, Brynn," Blake murmured so Tommy wouldn't hear. "She only wanted to lure you here, knowing you were a threat. To murder us all. All but Tommy."

I nodded, letting him know I understood.

It was no surprise. She didn't need all of us. She only needed to stop us from spoiling her vendetta. If she erased us, her descendants could rise again in strength and avenge her.

"We're all getting out of here," I stated. "Combining our powers, we can create a force she never knew existed."

Shane stepped closer, listening intently. "How?" he asked.

I didn't have an answer for him. I only had faith in what we were capable of doing. As a team.

"We need to attack her weakness. Strike terror into her heart and soul," I instructed. "Her family."

They all nodded, understanding our leverage.

Then a blood-curdling shriek pierced through the darkness from above, causing us all to turn at full attention.

"We need to strike now, while she's disoriented," I said. "She's unclear of what we are capable of right now. I've rattled her a bit."

Shane grinned. "Atta girl."

I smiled back and then moved toward the stairs. Poorva took Tommy's hand, and we climbed together.

The glow of our energy intensified as we connected with each other's thoughts, forming one single stream of consciousness.

With the force of an army, we burst through the cellar door and stormed into the witch's lair.

She stood tall in the center of the room and let out an unnerving cackle.

"So, you've found your friends," she laughed. "Weak fools. My hounds will tear you to shreds."

I stepped to the side, exposing Tommy.

She gasped, and her bony fingers flew to her blackened mouth.

"How dare you," she gasped, reaching for Tommy. "That's my boy."

"He's not your boy," I barked. "You stole him from someone else."

"She doesn't deserve him," she squealed. "That witch thinks she's the master of us. Always has. But she has no idea how to use her magic. A waste. She's a shame to us all."

My eyes widened.

Ms. Kelly was a witch. She was the leader of her sect.

Of course.

I'd seen it in her.

But now I realized the extent of her power and the level of the haters that surrounded her.

The Dark Witch was a defector.

They were arch enemies.

She moved closer to us, dragging her long, dark cloak behind her.

"Give me my boy," she said, reaching out with her bony fingers.

Tommy shrank behind us, shaking and whimpering.

In that instant, the energy of all of us gathered in my body, and I stepped forward.

My hands glowed purple as I reached them out to her. Power surged through my arms into my palms, and the purple hue grew into rising balls of flame.

The Dark Witch reeled back from the sight of it and stared in horror into the flickering fire.

With a hiss, she sneered, "Is that all you've got? Pathetic minions. She's taught you nothing."

And with that, she lurched forward, grabbing at Tommy with a twisted shriek.

Energy exploded from my palms as I threw my hands in her direction. Purple flames burst from me and enveloped her cloak in a roaring rush of fire.

She fell back, stumbling to the center of the room, screaming, as her entire cloak went up in flame. Screeching in pain, she pulled at her face as she burned.

"Run!" I shouted to the others.

We flew to the door and tore out of the house as boards and shutters dropped from its sides.

Her shrill screams followed us as she cried for Tommy.

"Bring back my boy," she sobbed. "My boy..." her voice trailed off in despair. Then in a final effort of resistance, she called out to her hounds. "Kill them!" She commanded. "All but my boy!"

The purple glow of flames shot out from every crevice in the boarded windows as her suffering streaked out with it. The entire house became engulfed in purple fire as we ran for our lives.

As we hit the twisted, gnarled branches of the surrounding woods, we struggled to get as far away as possible. But then, our ears filled with the sinister growling of her hounds, proving we'd never get away.

Low rumbling growls of the hound pack circled us as we pushed through the tangled branches. Their beady red eyes glowed in the surrounding darkness and outnumbered us by far. Closing in, they tightened together, preparing to pounce.

Their kill orders had been clear, and the sound of their snapping jaws confirmed they were ready to obey.

"They're about to attack," Blake cried out.

"Pull together," Shane commanded, grabbing sticks off the ground. He handed one to Blake and one to Poorva. "Aim for their snouts." He reached around on the ground, searching for more possible weapons.

My heart pounded in my chest, knowing we were outnumbered and out-clawed. There was no way we could fight off hell hounds, especially ones under the Dark Witch's spell.

"Weapons won't work," I shouted. "We need to use our powers instead."

"Like what?" Blake spat. "Read their thoughts to death."

His cynicism would have been amusing if we weren't facing a mauling, but in this moment, it didn't seem helpful. But then I thought about his comment more deeply. Could it be possible to read their minds or feel their emotions?

"Blake, try," I commanded. "Shane, see what you can feel from them."

They looked at each other for a brief moment and then turned to face the encroaching predators.

"They're hungry," Shane called out. "It's making them more agitated.

"They're divided," Blake added. "Their leader is missing."

"Perfect," I shouted. "We can create disorder for them, and without a leader, they'll struggle with their strategy. They'll tire quickly as well from the hunger. We have a chance!"

Poorva pulled Tommy closer. "If you lead them away from us, I'll be able to protect Tommy."

"Okay," Shane agreed. "We'll race in different directions and climb the first trees that are climbable. They'll jump endlessly to try to reach us. That will buy us the chance to escape when they need to rest."

"Let's do it," I called out. "Ready?"

"Go!" Blake shouted and tore into the thick of the trees.

Shane shot in a different direction, and I bolted in another.

The hounds split up instantly and pursued us, as Poorva and Tommy scrambled up a nearby tree.

The thick branches slowed the huge hounds, and they fought to break through them, giving us a small advantage. With no clear plan, they ran and clawed, expending all their energy without a unified purpose.

Before long, they fatigued and trailed behind each of us, panting. We circled back to Poorva and Tommy, calling them down from their tree.

"Now's our opening," Shane shouted.

With those words, the sound of a banshee's wail broke through the trees from the burning house.

"My boy!" the Dark Witch cried out.

Goosebumps rose on my arms at the sound of her wailing voice. She needed him and knew she'd meet her doom without his help. It was torturous to hear her calling his name, like the anguish of a grieving mother.

"Come on," I blasted to the others. "This way!"

We turned toward the direction of the portal and just as we started to sprint, the hounds returned. This time, they listened to the Dark Witch's strategy.

"Circle around," she commanded them. "Block them from gaining access to the gate. Then attack. Go for their throats."

Her voice sent them into a frenzy, and they moved as a unified pack. We'd tired them out, but their new organized approach gave them fresh energy.

"Keep running," I shouted. "We'll make it!"

We ran toward the portal, and before long, its tall, pointed structure shot into view.

"They're already there," Blake called out, seeing the hounds blocking its entrance.

The hounds created a terrifying blockade to the portal, with glaring death-eyes and snapping jowls.

"I want my mommy," Tommy cried. "Mommy!"

His words sent a vibration through the trees that wobbled everything around us. We slowed to regain our balance and stared at Tommy. His power was beyond anything we'd seen.

"Call out for her again," Shane encouraged him. "Make her hear you."

Tommy looked at him with a worried expression.

"Go ahead," Shane assured him.

"Mommy!" Tommy called out with a crack in his voice. "Mommy, help me!"

Like shattering glass, his voice exploded our minds and everything around us, sending resonating shock waves through our souls. Then the portal shook, causing the loose boards to rattle and break. With an eruption of sound, a voice burst out from the portal, hitting us all in our hearts.

"Tommy?" Ms. Kelly's broken voice cried out from another realm.

Ms. Kelly's consciousness had crossed over.

It seemed impossible, but it was true.

Her voice called out from the portal for Tommy as she searched for him through the transcendental abyss.

His psychic power had been able to connect them. And now, she was here on this side, with us.

The hounds growled and snapped as we got closer to the portal.

"Ms. Kelly," I cried. "We're almost there. But the hounds...."

Her voice filled my head. "You have the skill to overpower them, Brynn. Don't be afraid. Use it."

And with that, I squeezed my eyes shut and lifted my hands. The purple aura returned, and I focused harder until it shot up into flames.

Casting my hands in every direction, I blasted fireballs at each of the hounds, exploding flames on their bodies, causing them to yelp in pain. I continued throwing fire at them until they ran to escape the burning agony.

"Now!" I screamed to the others.

We flew into the tiny shack, and just as the hurricane-force winds began surrounding us, the sound of the Dark Witch caught us from behind as she cried, "My boyyyyyy..."

And then faded to black.

## CHAPTER 26

With a crash landing, we fell against the dirt floor of the triangular portal. We scrambled to our feet, brushing off the debris, and looked at each other with uncertainty.

Had we landed back in our realm or were the hungry hounds waiting just outside, ready to pounce on us.

Before any of us could say a word, Tommy cried out, "Mommy?"

I moved to the opening of the structure and peered out. A full moon shone its light across the clearing, and my eyes fell on a huge black wolf. At first, I thought it was one of the witch's hounds, but the size was much greater.

Dom.

He remained hovering over Laney, as her mother begged for him to leave her alone.

They were in the exact moment when we left them.

No time had passed.

Nothing had changed.

Except one thing.

Tearing across the field was a woman, running and stumbling across the grass.

"Tommy!" Ms. Kelly's voice shot in our direction.

I gasped in shock and turned to the others.

"Ms. Kelly's here," I shouted. "Tommy, your mother's here!"

Tommy pushed past the others and jumped to the opening of the hut. Looking out, he caught a glimpse of her running toward us. He barreled out of the portal and ran for her.

Tears poured from my eyes as I witnessed their heart-breaking, long-awaited reunion.

Shane pressed close to me and watched with equal amazement.

The two of them ran into each other's arms and embraced as if they were one.

Another figure raced from out of the trees toward them, and panic rose in me. Were they being attacked again? My fight response prepared itself.

But then, in an instant, my fear subsided as I focused on Minister Kelly. He wrapped his broad arms around the two of them, and together, they sobbed with tears of joy.

∼

As if frozen in time, we all stared as the Kelly's rejoiced.

My heart soared for them, and we all felt powerful gratitude for being a part of bringing them back together.

I turned to Shane to see how he was reacting to his friend's reunion with his parents. It must have been so strange for Shane, being seventeen, while his best friend from his childhood was still nine or ten. Time had slowed for Tommy, to what seemed like a matter of weeks for him, but it was years for everyone who missed and loved him.

The distant look in Shane's eye told me he was just as baffled by everything that had occurred. And quickly, the faraway look switched to one of emotional overload.

He turned to me and nearly collapsed into my arms. His trembling body heaved as quakes of sorrow mixed with relief shook out of him.

"It's okay, Shane," I whispered. "You found him."

"Finally," he murmured. "I wish it could have been sooner."

"All that matters is that he's here now. Safe." I held him close and allowed him to pour his battered soul into mine.

Just as we started to stand stronger, the sound of snapping wood jarred us. We shot our eyes to the triangular portal and watched as its wooden beams broke and crushed into themselves. The hut imploded with a mangled sound of breaking bones and crushing skulls. In a sudden whoosh of splinters and dust, the structure collapsed into itself and trailed off into the darkness of the woods.

It was gone.

"Thank you, Brynn," he sighed into my hair. "You made it all happen."

My eyes narrowed from his words. I still had no idea what my part in all of this was. My gifts had just recently unlocked, and now here I was, in the center of the most extreme occurrence of my life.

I prepared to deny his statement when I caught eyes with the wolf.

He stared at me with a confused expression. Shaking his head slightly and huffing, he pushed away from Laney. She scrambled out from under his hold and crawled closer to her mother. The wolf continued to stare at me as I held Shane close.

"Dom," I called to him.

But it was too late. He'd backed away from Laney and her mother, turned, and ran into the woods out of sight.

My heart plummeted as I stared after him into the darkness.

He had no idea what had just occurred. All he knew was what he saw in this moment. And now he was gone.

Then Laney's voice cried out. "Mother? Are you there?"

Her mother shimmied closer to her, confused at first by her question. But then her mother's face fell, and she too cried out. "Laney? I can't feel you."

"I can't feel you either, Mom," Laney screamed. "It's like your hidden from me. Blocked. What's happening?"

Her mother reached for her shoulders and shook her. "Try harder," she pleaded.

As they struggled to reconnect their powers to one another, my eyes shifted to the center of the clearing where Courtney stood.

She was no longer in flames. No longer suffering in agony.

She stood still, just watching.

She gazed upon Ms. Kelly and her family with a gentle smile across her lips. A tear rolled down her relaxed face.

Her head tipped then as she glanced in my direction. She sent me a soft nod of contentment.

She was at peace for the very first time.

# EPILOGUE

Emerging from the woods, we entered the lot where we'd initially gathered earlier in the evening. We huddled together, all of the UMAs—all except for Dom. He'd run into the woods, maybe to shift back into his human form in private, or perhaps to escape witnessing the new, stronger bond between Shane and me. I hoped he would be okay on his own out there.

As we watched Ms. Kelly and her family walk out of the woods, a car door slammed behind us. Out on the road, hidden from sight, someone approached our location, and we stared as the sound of crunching gravel resounded beneath each of their steps. Then he turned the corner into the lot—the school resource officer, Sargent Flynn.

He moved straight for Ms. Kelly, and we all stood taller, ready to defend her.

As he approached, his eyes fell on Tommy, and he stopped in his tracks.

Ms. Kelly took Tommy's hand and walked him over to the officer.

"Tommy." She leaned down to her son. "Do you remember Sargent Flynn?"

Tommy nodded. "Uh-huh. He has the cool police dog."

Sargent Flynn laughed. "That's right, young man. You're Trooper's favorite cadet."

He glanced at Ms. Kelly, clearly rattled by the fact that Tommy was found, and was the same age as when he went missing. His K9, Trooper, was likely long gone by now, but he didn't have the heart to tell the boy. He stepped closer to Ms. Kelly and whispered in her ear, though I could still hear him perfectly.

"I wouldn't believe it if I didn't see it with my own eyes," he said. "Forgive me for not believing sooner."

She placed her hand on his shoulder. "It's unbelievable, Dave. But you had enough faith to get us here at lightning speed. Thank you."

He nodded and turned to Minister Kelly, shaking his hand.

I glanced at Shane, and he had the same surprised look in his eye as me. Sargent Flynn had driven the Kelly's here in his cruiser, probably with the lights and siren blaring. He had known something extraordinary was happening that required his assistance. He just would never know the exact explanation behind it all.

Then all eyes shot to the opening of the trail as movement caught our attention.

Laney and her mother hobbled out of the woods with their heads down, avoiding eye contact with anyone.

Sargent Flynn approached them. "Mrs. Rosco. You are under arrest. We have reason to believe you were involved in the disappearance of Tommy Kelly. There is evidence that points to the obstruction of justice. You'll need to be questioned at the...."

Ms. Rosco crumpled to her knees as Laney acted surprised, shooting accusations of mistrust at her.

"Mother? How could you?" Her feigned shock didn't trick anyone.

Laney and her mother had already lost all credibility in this town.

Sargent Flynn's voice trailed off while he continued to explain Mrs. Rosco's rights to her, and we all gathered around Ms. Kelly and her family.

It was unbelievable. Sargent Flynn had no idea how any of this was possible, but it was clear he was on Ms. Kelly's side. He would be the one to clear her name.

I stepped back from the excitement that surrounded the Kelly's and dropped down on one of the benches. Staring into the woods, I rubbed my hands through my hair, trying to absorb the magnitude of what had occurred.

"You good?" Shane's voice soothed my frayed nerves as he sat next to me.

I turned to him and smiled. "Yeah. I'm good." I glanced at Tommy. "You?"

He shrugged. "I don't know. A bit traumatized, probably."

"Yeah. Makes sense," I huffed. "It might take a bit for us to recover from this one."

I pressed on the bridge of my nose, squinting my eyes.

Shane reached over and took my wrist. "What's that?" he asked, pushing my sleeve higher.

With a gasp, I stared at a strange marking on my inner forearm. It looked like a burn, but there was no pain. The star shape was intricate and mesmerizing.

Shane shot his eyes over to Ms. Kelly, and in an instant, she was at my side examining my arm.

She stared at the mythical design without speaking and then glanced back toward the woods with a harrowed look in her eyes.

"What is it?" Shane asked.

Ms. Kelly turned back to me, still holding my wrist.

"It's the ancient mark of the witch hunter," she said, staring into my eyes.

She recoiled slightly, unsure of how I would respond, but I had no clue what it could mean.

Fear churned in her eyes as she gazed at me.

Being called a witch hunter didn't frighten me. If anything, it clarified my existence. It made clear my purpose, and I immediately felt its strength within me.

"Ms. Kelly, you're safe with me," I assured her. "If I'm a witch hunter, then it's only those who practice dark magic that I will pursue."

Her shoulders relaxed as she nodded. Her belief in me allowed us to reconnect as master and student.

"Well then," she started. "We have a new focus. A new mission."

My eyes widened, and Shane sat taller at full attention.

She continued, "The Dark Witch will return. She always does." She paused, glancing at the rest of the UMAs. They noticed her call and gathered around us. "A+ on your first project, students. But there's no time to waste basking in your success. Now, you must prepare for your next assignment."

We all stared at each other as our excitement mounted.

Ms. Kelly looked at each of us with pride in her eyes and stated, "Second project, capture the Dark Witch."

<<<<>>>>

I hope you enjoyed book one
**URBAN MYSTIC ACADEMY: FIRST PROJECT**
Please take a moment to leave a brief review in hopes of helping others find this series.

Read ahead for a sample of book two
**Urban Mystic Academy: Second Project**

ALSO BY JENNIFER ROSE MCMAHON

**URBAN MYSTIC ACADEMY SERIES**
Urban Mystic Academy: First Project
Urban Mystic Academy: Second Project
Urban Mystic Academy: Third Project

**ASYLUM SAVANT SERIES**
The Shuttered Ward, Book One
The Excited Ward, Book Two
The Forgotten Ward, Book Three

**IRISH MYSTIC LEGENDS SERIES**
Legend Hunter, Book One
Curse Raider, Book Two
Truth Seer, Book Three

**PIRATE QUEEN SERIES**
Bohermore, Book One
Inish Clare, Book Two
Ballycroy, Book Three
Rockfleet, Prequel (best read as Book 2.5)

# ABOUT THE AUTHOR

Jennifer Rose McMahon is a USA Today Bestselling Author who has been creating her stories since her college days abroad in Ireland. Her passion for urban legends, ancient cemeteries, abandoned asylums, and medieval ghost stories has fueled her adventurous storytelling, while her husband's decadent brogue carries her imagination through the centuries. When she's not writing about castles and curses, she can be found near Boston in the local coffee shop, yoga studio, or at the beach…most often answering to the name 'Mom' by her fab children four.

Keep turning to read a free sample of Book Two, **URBAN MYSTIC ACADEMY: SECOND PROJECT**

Be sure to visit my website for more information about my other books.
www.jenniferrosemcmahon.com

To sign up for my newsletter:
https://www.subscribepage.com/f1p9w6

# SAMPLE-URBAN MYSTIC ACADEMY: SECOND PROJECT

Supposedly, returning to school after completing the first project would be epic. Our powers would be tweaking after being put to the ultimate test and we'd be more bonded than ever. We'd finally be able to act normal again and integrate back into the student body like the regular kids. But that turned out to be the farthest thing from the truth.

Maybe it was the distraction of my new pink hair that derailed the heightened celebration.

Or maybe it was the fact that Ms. Kelly was still absent and the gossip mill had churned out more rumors about her alleged misconduct than we could count.

But the stares and whispers in the hallways had reached an all time high, reminding me that nothing had changed. It had only become worse.

The pink hair shouldn't have been such a big deal. I mean, the purple version was far more intense. I always changed the color just as I was about to transition to something new, so the timing felt natural, almost like a rebirth. And I'd never gone the pink route before, it always seemed too optimistic, proving that I'd likely become overly eager. My impatience may have caused a bit of a back-fire.

I brushed off the judging glares and bombed toward my first-period class. Seeing Dom would ground me again, especially since Laney would be on the absent list for quite a while. Her world had turned upside-down not only when her powers became blocked but more so as her mother had her rights read and was taken away by the police. I felt bad for a milli-second but remembered quickly the evil the Roscos were capable of.

I shuddered at the thought of how they had hurt the town of Lakefield. Their hate and vengeance ran deep and laced every breath they took.

It made sense to me now, though.

At first, I thought Laney was a queen-bee-bitch for the fun of it—destroying teen lives at every turn. But after meeting her ghostly ancestor who'd been burned at the stake in Hell's Gates—now caught in limbo, and feeding off the souls of local children—I had new perspective on her royal bitchiness.

Turning into my AP Lit class, I scanned the room for Dom, looking forward to seeing him for the first time since he tore off into the woods of Hell's Gates in his wolf form. He'd been out of touch all weekend and I worried that he was struggling with his new 'situation'. I'm sure bursting into a wolf was not on his high school bucket list. It probably was the last thing he thought even possible, and likely had him pretty freaked out.

I wouldn't blame him. Seeing him transform into an enormous snarling wolf had rattled me, but not as much as I would have expected. It was almost like I anticipated it. He'd demonstrate several wolf-like tendencies, but more so, it was the heat and energy that radiated off him that warned me something was about to explode.

And not to mention, there was something seriously hot about it.

Gazing through the rows of desks, I searched for Dom as the late bell rang. Everyone took their seats as Mr. Benson, the Senior Slayer, marched into the room with a look of determination that he'd teach us the classics whether we liked it or not. I took my seat before being told to, and stared at Dom's empty desk.

## URBAN MYSTIC ACADEMY: FIRST PROJECT

*

Seeing Poorva at our lab station in physics sent relief through my bones. My imagination had run away with me while I sat through Mr. Benson's droning lecture in Lit class. I worried that maybe I was the only UMA who'd made it to school that day. I panicked that something or someone had gotten to some of us, pulling us away from each other. It was deep-seeded fear that we all share.

And now, I couldn't help but worry about Dom. It made no sense that he wasn't here in school.

"Poorva," I gasped. "I'm so glad you're here."

"Of course I am," she said. "I wouldn't miss it. The next school day after completing a project is the best and most important. We all get to recount everything that happened and we pull together the final report. It's always super energy charged and exciting." Her bright eyes flashed as she checked the clock. "One more hour," she stated.

"But Dom's not here," I blurted. "He wasn't in Lit."

Her expression shifted in an instant as her brows pulled in. "What?"

"He's not here, Poorva."

Her pensive silence worried me as she pulled her hand through her long black hair. "Where could he be?" she murmured. "It makes no sense."

Setting up our ramp for our acceleration and velocity lab, we fumbled our way through the project while remaining focused on only one thing—Dom's absence.

"Did he ever come out of the woods?" Poorva asked. "Did anyone notice or see him after that?"

"I have no idea," I whispered. "I think in the excitement of it all, we each did our own form of recovery yesterday."

"Like, the hair?" She took the ends of my pink hair and rubbed them. "It looks amazing. Almost not real."

"Yeah, it's kind of what I do when something big is happening," I huffed. "Like a coping mechanism, I guess."

She grinned. "Well, I like it." She lifted her hands to me and showed me her bit-off nails. "This is my coping mechanism. Not quite as pretty."

"Seems like that's a natural response," I said, setting up our lab station, wondering what all the bits were for.

She rolled the tennis ball in thought. "So, Dom and Courtney were the only ones who didn't text in the group yesterday. It didn't seem unusual at the time," she mumbled in concentration. "I just assumed Dom would be embarrassed or confused by what happened to him. And Courtney never replies, either way."

"I wondered that about Dom, too," I agreed. "Behind all the bravado, he's actually really sensitive. Maybe he just couldn't get out of bed today." I discreetly checked my phone for any new texts.

As we focused on rolling the tennis ball down our makeshift ramp, we recorded the speed-data blindly. The students around us chattered about their results, making predictions about their next roll, but Poorva and I sat in silence, waiting impatiently for the bell.

Our teacher moved from station to station, checking on each team's progress. Poorva rushed our conclusion onto the data collection sheet as I disassembled the lab. Just as Dr. Corley approached our bench, a strange sound filled my mind and I shot my eyes to Poorva.

Her hand smacked over her mouth as she listened harder. Our eyes locked onto each other as we focused on the eerie sound.

Dr. Corley's voice morphed around us as he attempted to gain our attention. "Your results are...."

Hum. Buzz. Bur. His words whirled around us, finding no way in.

But the sound in our heads, it grew more clear as we stared at each other in silence.

"My boy....," a cracking voice grated through our minds.

I reached for Poorva and grabbed her arms. Her rapid breathing proved she was hearing the same thing.

"Girls, are you okay?" Dr. Corley's voice broke into our circle.

"My boy....," the cackle grew louder.

I crouched, pressing my hands over my ears with a wince. "No!" I blasted.

Poorva stepped back covering her ears, as well, and shaking her head. "Stop!" she cried.

The voice grew louder, calling to us. "I hear you. I feel you," it said. "Return him to me. I won't rest until he's returned."

I pulled Poorva away from the lab station and ran toward our desks. We grabbed our backpacks and stumbled toward the door.

"Yes, to the nurse," Dr. Corley called to us with a shaking voice. "Or to the counseling office, whichever...."

We fell into the hall and bombed away from the classroom, looking back to be sure the Dark Witch wasn't on our tails. Her evil voice shot terror into our souls and our natural response was to run.

Turning the corner down the C wing, we smashed into another student running in our direction.

"Blake!" I gasped.

Then Shane and Courtney barreled around the corner with the same look of terror in their eyes.

We huddled tight together in the hall, gasping for air.

"What the fuck?" Shane blasted. "Fuck!"

Staring wildly at each other, waiting for the next assault on our senses, we jumped as the bell rang.

"Come on," I said, ushering them to follow. "To the guidance suite!"

\*

We stormed the guidance suite and threw our packs in every direction. Pulling chairs over to the center table, we squished in around it and let out a collective exhale.

"Isn't this supposed to be the part when we regale our success story and celebrate our awesomeness?" Shane snarked.

Everyone remained silent, as if anticipating another bone-chilling assault on our senses from the dark witch.

I glanced across the table at Courtney. Her eyes were wide as saucers, but she was interacting and emoting like the rest of us.

"Courtney, you're back," I whispered.

Her hair wisped away from her face, exposing a restful gaze. The grimace of pain and suffering had been wiped away, allowing for her to talk with us now. It was a huge win from the first project.

She nodded with a slight smile, likely still getting used to the fact that she finally wasn't burning from the inside out. Her gruesome torture had finally subsided.

But Shane was right, there was no rejoicing at the moment. We were still being threatened and had no time to sit back and party.

Then our heads shot in the same direction as a jarring voice pulled our attention toward the offices.

"Ms. Damien will supervisor your advisory group while I determine how you'll be reassigned." Principal Haney's voice punched us in our faces.

Ms. Damien glared at us like we were an inconvenience to her day. How a school secretary could remain employed after proving her distain for students over and over was beyond me.

Principal Haney scanned our group and I caught a glimpse of uncertainty in her eyes. Or was it fear?

I turned to Shane and he lifted his brows at me. He had seen her apprehension too.

"When will Ms. Kelly be back?" Blake called out.

My spine stiffened as I glared at him for bringing her up so soon.

We had no idea if she would be returning.

Her cause for dismissal would likely be reversed, particularly when Sargent Flynn got a chance to clear her name, but convincing Principal Haney of her innocence would be the next hurdle. And judging by the way she glared at us, it would be a monumental task.

But we needed Ms. Kelly.

It would be awful if we were separated and sent to new advisory groups. We needed the face-to-face time with Ms. Kelly, and her group activities, in order to continue our growth. Her mentorship was what got us this far. I could only imagine how much more we could grow if she were here with us.

We sat in silence, refusing to allow Ms. Damien to overhear our conversations. Her watchful gaze proved she was hoping to gather any information possible to add to her gossip circles. Even in our silence, she was probably collecting details to spin through the rumor mill—something like, "They're so odd. Sitting in silence staring at each other. Freaks."

It didn't matter what she thought, though. And those who listened to her tales, they weren't worth it either. But why did it have to be so hard to convince myself that the judgers didn't matter? I groaned in annoyance.

Shane laughed at my response to Ms. Damien's presence.

Then Courtney chuckled.

The tension of the moment relaxed some and once Blake and Poorva let out giggles, we lost it.

We laughed out loud until tears rolled down our faces. The release was beyond cathartic as we hunched over, holding our stomachs in ab-crunching guffaws.

After a few more seconds, we settled down, gasping for air. Ms. Damien stared at us like we were crazy and tapped away on her phone, texting whoever would listen to her rant about us.

Just as we regained our composure, a voice entered our silent circle.

"I'm glad to see you are all together again," the voice said. "But one is missing?"

Ms. Kelly!

Our eyes shot wide and we stared at each other, straining to hear every word. We darted our gazes around to be sure we all were hearing it. Our piqued reactions made it clear we were.

I sucked in air and held it, listening intently.

"Ms. Kelly?" I channeled my thoughts to her.

In an explosion, everyone's voices joined mine at a silent, focused point above our table. The space opened in our minds, allowing for all of our voices to be heard without any of us making a sound. Our collective consciousness was in tact, even without Dom, and Ms. Kelly was able to access it.

"Yes, hello students," Ms. Kelly said. "I'm very proud of all of you and will never be able to thank you enough. You've accomplished your first project with amazing skill, exceeding my expectations ten-fold."

We remained silent, listening to her every word.

She continued. "However, it is not over. I sense danger within your circle. There's an evil presence."

My breath whooshed out of me, along with the other's.

Blake's voice rose above. "It's the same one I'd felt before. It's able to enter our thoughts."

Silence hovered in our thoughts as insidious fear creeped through us like venom.

We knew we were in danger.

The Dark Witch was still among us and Ms. Kelly sensed it too.

Just as the bell was about to ring, ending advisory period, she added, "It is not over, students, and therefore, without much opportunity for rest, I must help focus you. It is time." She paused. "Time to assign the second project."

**Urban Mystic Academy: Second Project**

Made in the USA
Las Vegas, NV
28 February 2022